When M. Miller, slide librarian at a large Seattle stock photo agency, falls asleep in a rep cinema one rainy autumn evening, she finds the dead invading her dreams, a mysterious stranger talking about her past, & her job taking on sudden, strange, suspicious dimensions.

With the help of Kurt Cobain, François Villon, & the agency's own Leather Boys, she slips past the Space Needle to confront love, death, resurrection, & globalization.

praise for **Seattle:** a novella

Bartleby the Scrivener is alive, unwell, and re-living the gloomy doomy in the form of McAuliffe's brooding, misanthropic, rain-spat heroine. Impotent rage cohabitates with brilliantly arch condemnations to salt this unmoored yet claustrophobic tale.

— Kassten Alonso, author, *Core (a Miaden)*, *& The Pet Thief*

A marvelous stretch of work.

— Matthew Stadler, author, *Deventer*, *The Dissolution of Nicholas Dee*, *Chloe Jarren's La Cucaracha*, *& Where We Live Now;* Publication Studio co-founder

Praise for Seattle: a novella

Back office transactions, cavernous electronic databases, suspicious dealings, duplicity, innocence, the complexities of lost love ... The controlled rage throughout *Seattle* does the memory of Mother Jones proud.

— Julie Madsen, editor, *W**O*R*K** * Magazine

praise for SEATTLE: a novella

M.F. McAuliffe's *Seattle* tells the story of a bereft widow and disillusioned photographer working as a librarian at an image agency. Amid the digitally strained commerce of a photojournalism company her secretive impressions and fragmentary memories streak through the prose in poetic bursts of tension, anger and doubt. The nervous power of the writing is reminiscent of old style photography, when film would be processed in developer so that a latent image could become visible. One feels the story beneath Seattle emerging with the same chemical intensity, its meaning rising before you moment by moment.

— Mark Mordue, author, *Dastgah: Diary of A Head Trip*

Seattle:
a novella

M. F. McAuliffe

a shoegaze book

SHOEGAZE BOOKS ISBN 978-1-94424441-5

$12.00

(Also available in a Digital Edition,

pub. Sept., 2015, ISBN 978-1-943843-27-5)

||| Cover & Interior Design: T. Warburton y Bajo ||| Int. red star youth images: T. Warburton y Bajo ||| Cover & Interior: Var. Seattle Space Needle landscape image elements: Nathan Tompkins |||

10 9 8 7 6 5 4 3 2

SEATTLE:

a novella

M. F. McAULIFFE

SEATTLE: A NOVELLA

1st. print ed., 2nd printing, pub. Nov., 2015, Shoegaze Books,

distrib. by GobQ L.L.C., 338 NE Roth, Portland OR 97211

For

JAS, BV, & GKW

who have sustained me with friendship

& for

RVB

without whom there would have been nothing to sustain

(sept. 1993 — nov. 1997)

(i)

On Thursday nights she left her long internal dialogue for the promises of the Grand Illusion.

It was dark, bitter, raining. She was at the pictures. She had turned sideways in her seat. Her overcoat covered her shoulder. Images the colour of moonscape began to move and merge across the screen.

She had been free for a moment. Between escaping from the Iron Triangle and then from Adelaide, she had betrayed another runaway, like her. Left the boy to fend for himself while she escaped from Adelaide and Oz, Greece and California. She'd abandoned him. Worse. Left him to the cops.

She had been free for another moment. And in that moment Rypdal had interviewed her.

It had been a cheerful interview. Edgy, but cheerful.

"Political photographs then?"

"Not necessarily. Not overtly."

"Walker Evans?"

"Mm. Herman Leonard."

"Eugene Smith."

"His wife. Or that Soviet war photographer. Survived Stalin. Peasant women on the battlefield going from body to body, trying to identify the dead."

"Dimitri Nikolaevich Baltermants, born Warsaw 1912. *Tchaikowsky*. Four Russian soldiers in a bombed-out building."

"Berlin, 1945."

"One soldier playing an upright piano, a thick pottery jar of flowers standing on the top. Soldiers outlined in light. Great shot. Great propaganda."

"I hate it. The hanging roof-beam for ruination, light for hope, music for Russian soul conquering German iron. Soul doesn't conquer anything; it just fails to be completely destroyed, sometimes. That photo's hokey and stagey and all hot air. It's calculated. It *truckles*. But the one with the dead soldier on the icy road, from early in the war, that one I'd buy. It's the whole ball of wax, everyone's deepest dread, dying alone and desolate and very probably for nothing. Which was exactly why Stalin wouldn't print it. But in the first one you mentioned, where the women are bent over the bodies, whatever Baltermants might have done about arranging the composition, the death was still real."

"*Grief*." Rypdal had paused, fixed her with intense sea-green eyes. "A hundred and seventy six thousand Soviet casualties, soldiers and civilians."

He'd looked at her, paused again.

"The women were looting."

She had no idea whether he was joking. His eyes glittered; the lower half of his face was a golden barrage of stubble. She felt her temples begin to throb. The woman in the background had been doubled over. The woman in the foreground was bent, hands clasped. About to loot? Having just looted? The woman could have been in the throes of horror and loss, the woman could have been faking. From within the photo itself, as far as she could remember it, there was no way to tell.

She couldn't challenge Rypdal's ferocious glitter. She still suffered from the naïveté that had always been her basic assumption and starting point.

She had to say something into the silence.

"I suppose I've — The world might not be — Well, of course it isn't, or hasn't. It just never used to be quite so — It just never used to be quite that dangerously different, perhaps. From peoples' assumptions."

The assumptions of the peasants. The thousands upon thousands of bodies, the war. Of course the world had been different. Stalin, Hitler, the species itself had seen to it.

"Well, post-War."

Rypdal didn't react. She waited for the judgement implicit in his next words. Naïveté wouldn't do in a stock agency.

Waited.

She couldn't afford to wait any longer. She had to try and retrieve some credibility.

"S'pose the death of the photographer's the only way of underwriting the authenticity of the work. In combat, anyway. And maybe not always then."

Rypdal said nothing. His eyes opaque.

"Larry Burrows."

The words hardly seemed to have come from the man. It was obviously a last chance; she had to say something seriously sensible, if not arrestingly apt.

"Good work. No imperatives except from within the image. Frank Hurley. Damien Parrer."

The stubble may have smiled. Ah, she thought, a name he hasn't heard for a while.

"So what else do you like? Apart from death and destruction. Avedon? Mapplethorpe?"

"Fashion's not really my thing, I'm afraid."

Eyes a clear green sea. "What's the most important feature of a good stock image?"

"Good negative space. Plenty of blank bits for the copy to go in."

"Right the first time."

As she was leaving she'd turned back on impulse, grinned. "Bourke-White. The father of photojournalism."

He'd grinned back, an astounding flash that lit up the room. "Wish she'd been mine."

For a while it had become their catch-all greeting.

Rypdal's sleeveless vest and its bulky, flapping pockets made him loom large, but she realized, as her first week's training went on, he was actually thin. The ferocity of his focus left her awed and fearful. Though she waited for him to find her inadequate and let her go he didn't seem to find that a priority.

She puzzled, worried.

She still had the Institute's aging diploma. There had been the group shows, the attempts at art sale.

She'd finally concluded that though employees could place up to ten images in the company's files and she'd thanked Rypdal for the information and told him she'd put some of her images in, he saw her as neither a client nor a potential customer: she wasn't a photographer who'd rise or fall on vision, energy, the constant, vigorous, brilliant practice of a profession. She was a clerk. She was a loyal and perfectly adequate clerk with years of library experience and a basic grasp of the concepts.

But down the years she and Rypdal still grinned at each other if he were in town, the building, the corridor, if he had registered her presence, almost as though he recognized a parity between them. She'd never figured out what it could be. She left herself to decide, or not, between his manners, his delight in their common wit, and the glance he'd cast at the portfolio she'd sent in with her application.

By the end of the week she was weary to her bones.

When she was taking photos her bones were hollow; she was everywhere and nowhere, a weightless point, unseeing, allseeing; she was air and not an eye.

She took photos at night or over the weekend, in the early mornings of spring or autumn. She photographed light: the sky sliced by light, leaves, trees, rocks; cityscapes edged or surfaced with that northern light that always remembered the ice behind the sky, that ice-light that stayed almost into high summer, after the orange light of halloween and the lead light of early winter. She sold images sporadically; some years three or four, some years one or two, once a sequence to be sandwiched into the background on an REM album cover. More lately she hadn't sold any at all.

She didn't mention the sales; everyone at the

agency was selling images or grinding away with guitars at gigs. But the sales made her secretly one of them, a real photographer, who could almost, almost touch the light she saw. A photographer and not a clerk, finally fit to have married Tom, come here. *Coin of the realm*, the Institute had said, *the tribute paid to the professional.*

When the cheques came she'd spend them, get Orphan a couple of ounces of good fillet, replace a jacket or price a set of tyres. After she saw Rypdal's slide of the Indonesian sweatshop girl she started sending donations to Third World education programmes. On the strength of the REM sale she bought a decent watch; on days when she needed armour she wore the watch to work.

But the sales were never followed by diminishing response-times, vaguely friendly notes, enquiries, or commissions. After each one she seemed to begin again from scratch. Queries, sorting, getting a mailing together began to take Sisyphean amounts of effort; her body seemed less able or willing to move; she began to realize just how constantly her feet and back and shoulders ached.

She half-comically wondered if it was because

she had suspicions about the word *submit* — to bow the head; to request and thereby trigger the answer *no;* to accept and confirm the existing structures of power and powerlessness as though that confirmation, as much as working for free on weekends, were the true desire and fruit of media empires.

She also half-seriously wondered if the new weight and slowness of her movements were the sly, insidious beginnings of age.

Her credits could have been achieved by any amateur in a lifetime of mad and misconceived persistence.

The thought went through her like a guilt, a shame, a malevolent truth. It was late. She was late. She hadn't done anything, she found herself thinkingfeelingsaying to herself when she was tired. And she was almost always tired.

She turned, moved her other hip into the other corner of the seat, and settled again. Her neck ached. Her shoulder was cold.

(ii)

She had been free for a moment.

Her father had died; the money from her share of the estate had sat for a moment in a savings account, cash, liquid, potential. It could have become anything: drugged-out weekends in spectacularly sordid Hollywood hotels, languorous sessions with perfumed oils and gigolos, small-plane trips to the summit of Everest, safaris to the Amazon rainforest or the plains of Patagonia. It was not, she had decided, for returning to Oz. If she were a foreigner here she would be, as far as she could tell from furtive glances at *The Age* and *The Sydney Morning Herald* on the pc at work, even more foreign in Oz; unfashionably old, computer-illiterate, accent a bland pan-Commonwealth murmur. She'd go down like a lead balloon.

In reality, in the world of dirt and stones, the inheritance had become the downpayment on a small condo, a place slightly apart from the shadowy presences of landlord and supervisor, paycheque and eviction. The condo could be collateral; it could be sold, it could unburden her. It was an actual breathing-space and another potential freedom. But it was small; selling it would only set her free for another small, unsettled, unsettling moment.

But on Thursday nights she gave herself hope as a present, she anticipated the end of the workweek and the promise of semifreedom at the Grand Illusion, rep cinema to the low-income and film-school set. She went as much for the audience as for the movie, for the gentler, more tolerant nest-mate sounds people made as they settled into the dimness; she went to be in the dimness, to be as good as anyone else for as long as the movie lasted.

And her eyes were always tired. She'd rest her eyes, she'd tell herself, speaking almost as though her father were there, using his phrase and voice. Just rest her eyes.

She always went to sleep. In the close, confined air stiff and thick with the congealing smell of fake butter on instant corn, she drifted off, the back of her head on the backrest of the seat or her hip and knee and shoulder turned sideways to the screen. In the bitterest months she draped her overcoat from her shoulder. When the coat with its thermal linings slid off she felt the loss as fragility.

(iii)

It was dark and bitter, raining; it was the week before Thanksgiving. She was at the pictures. Her coat had slipped from her shoulder.

Her father was alive.

He was talking, brown suit, white hair, laughing. He wasn't ill. They were having a conversation. They were happy until she turned aside, uneasy, knowing something was wrong. As she turned he became an image and the image excluded her. The thin young man who was her father played with his giggling toddler on a black and white lawn. The black and white parent and child rounded out and laughed and went on throwing a big rubber ball.

They were alive. Her father was alive. She was an abstracted, unliving ghost.

She woke up startled, sweating, terrified, pulled her coat to her and turned to goosepimples under it.

She was a ghost. She was unreal. The thought was already in her skin.

Her mind couldn't tell life from death.

She was in a narrowing vortex of cold. There was no end but extinction.

She looked around. The strangers all had their own realities.

She stood and stumbled over everybody's feet, paused to stuff her arms into her coat, pushed herself through the winding, shabby-plush corridors and out into the thick, cold air and the battering of a heavy rain. She got to the nearest coffee-shop, stood blinking and dripping in the pallor of the moss-green and white and black neon sign. She shivered again, wished again that the place had never changed hands, wrestled with her wet coat, wiped her face with a napkin, ordered a tall mocha. She put her elbows on one of the small, repro-Scandinavian laminate tables, peeled the end of her sleeve back from her wrist and began to keep an eye on the time.

The pallor of the laminate was an essay in aloofness and dislocation.

But she was very carefully not thinking about it, she reminded herself; she would keep her mental distance from that sudden dark marsh where the dead slid into life and her daytime self slid into the dark unbreathing planes of death. She would not think. She would watch the interior of the shop reflected in its windows where the dark ground of the night and the weak neon of the room turned everything grey, watery, substanceless.

Her order was called. She collected it and sat holding the tall porcelain warmth of the cup. She closed her eyes, turned the warmth at her hands into billowing images of white. Comforter, doona, duvet, eiderdown, quilt: different words for the same means of warmth arising in different regions.... She drank and let fluttering bedclothes arrange themselves into a vague white circumpolar map while she said to the swamp her mind still wanted to become: *You dreamt about a photo. That's all. You dreamt about a photo.*

It had been one of a bundle her brother had sent.

She tried to see into her body, the self that operated in dark and liquid and osmosis. *Only a photo*. She repeated the phrase, trying to drain the swamp of fear that had spread and replaced all her normal processes.

"Excuse me."

She jumped.

A stranger was at her table, talking: the same grey, dark-grounded water-man who'd come into the window version of the shop after her and had stood behind her and looked at the menu while she'd been ordering.

"We've got these in Australia," gesturing at the repro-Scand and the corporate logo, "so I thought I'd come in."

She didn't give a damn about the state of cappuccino in Australia. The shop was just about empty. There was no reason for him to be here, the largest object in her vicinity, demanding her attention.

"Your accent," he said. "So I was wondering if I should say hello to a fellow countryman."

"I avoid Australians." The types, the stereotypes, the dull yellow ache of the map, what she'd seen of the hard-shelled, calculating young. She wanted to be left alone to deal with the swamp that had swallowed her.

But the stranger had put his briefcase and umbrella down, spread the umbrella to drip on the floor and was getting his wallet; he was wrestling with his raincoat, a thick, grey-brown, winter-coloured thing he was trying to hang on the back of his chair. She eyed the coat with malice.

"I'll be going in a minute." It was a lie. She hadn't intended to. But she would.

But he was moving the other chairs, spreading the coat there. He hadn't heard.

Any Australian in Seattle would be working for Gates or Murdoch, she guessed; God knew there was no one else to work for. Dear Rupert or Dear Bill, Gog or Magog… These days she remembered the dreams from her worst nights; woke in a tangle of legs and blankets under the tumble of the new bright twin rivers, Internet and Broadcast. They flowed from some mysterious origin in heaven, tinkling and sparkling; they fell with animated spangles around a cave of nonexistence. The cave was the home of grief and impotence and failure. The sea outside it was leather. It was the dry, mouth-filling sensation of leather that woke her.

"Excuse me," the stranger said. A smile and nod as he left.

For a moment she was dismayed at producing a desire this effortlessly; it usually meant she'd been indictably rude. But he was collecting a cappuccino, coming back with his cup and saucer and two packets of raw sugar.

Her heart rose at an implicit *not guilty* and then sank again. She thought of moving to another table. But if she moved there was no guarantee he wouldn't just raise his voice and converse from a distance. Or follow. In the side window she still looked grey and ghostly. If she moved she'd have to face herself. If she could just have been judiciously rude, she thought, or if she could just cohabit with the chatter without having to actually look or listen —

The stranger resettled, shook one of the sugar packets, tore the top left-hand corner and emptied the crystals onto the foam on the right-hand side of his cup.

She waited.

Nothing.

She waited again. The stranger began shaking the second packet from the top left-hand corner.

"So how come you're in Seattle? Do you live here? Do you work for Mic — "

"Something like that." He tore a small opening just below the pressure-crimped seal.

She wanted to disdain him, ignore this physical manifestation with its provincialism and its coat. Gossip and Lies were the only two industries left in the entire western world. Boeing was sliding into Asia or history as surely as the century was sliding into the millennium and Seattle and all who sailed in her sliding into poverty or the sea. He had nothing to say to her.

She would have glared at him, but he wasn't watching. He was making a second mound of sugar on the foam in his cup.

He looked up and smiled.

"I'm an agent. There's a film deal here and I'm representing my client."

"Oh."

"You're Australian. You might have heard of him. Stephen Black."

She didn't have time to be annoyed at his presumption; she felt as though a tide-edge of acid had washed some layer off her skin and revealed the hinges of her bones. But the name meant nothing. She couldn't attach it to any of Thursday afternoon's lobby-posters or Friday night's checkout stand tabloids.

"He does a lot of television now, locally-produced soaps, but he did quite a lot of theatre just after he graduated from NIDA. Some Shakespeare in London and then new Irish work in Dublin. He was from Yorkshire, originally."

She put on a vague, bland expression, nodded vaguely, and stared into the middle distance. She suddenly realized she'd never really forgotten how to have a conversation in Strine, how to make non-committal noises by way of gentle discouragement, glance inquiringly and often into the free space beyond.

This was their mutual heritage, she thought, sourly.

" — and he'd been living in the Iron Triangle,

of all places. Ran away, hitched a ride — "

She tried to command the dark regions under her skin, but her tired, uncommandable body wouldn't relinquish its hope or dread or excitement or alarm.

" — with one of his teachers. It was quite a yarn by the time — "

"Sorry? *Who* did you say?"

But she already understood. The man had just laid out all of his life and all of hers, and even her fiercest, most focused focus couldn't make the stranger's voice undo chance and causation.

The stranger dabbed at a thin line of foam on his lip. "One of his teachers."

"No, the kid."

"Stephen Black."

"What year was this?"

"Seventy-four."

Iron Triangle. Television. Actor. Happy ending, and she herself part of *quite a yarn*. A thin, curling, licking liquid edge and roll of pleasure began at her toes.

Something she'd done had had consequences, and twenty-five years later they were simultaneously across a table from her and flashing gaudily around the edges of another continent.

She wasn't a swamp of dissolution at all. She was alive. She was a shimmer of water on sand.

"D'he ever say who the teacher was?" Oh, shimmering, liquid sky.

The stranger picked up the slim wooden stick off his saucer, put it down, went back to the counter, fossicked in the trays, picked out a plastic spoon, and returned.

"No, Stephen never said. I didn't ask, there was too much else going on." He scooped at the remnants of froth in the cup's shallow curves. "The main part of his tale was about running away from his parents and the police."

A hand encircling a notebook.

Huge.

"Older woman. That's the only impression I had." His eyes looked from the empty spoon and cup, looked at her suddenly. "Why?"

She could go on shimmering, she thought, if time stopped.

But time never stopped. She was being pulled onward, dragged by the stranger's silence. His eyes and silence were remote and opaque and grey.

She shifted, looked down, forced her thumb and forefinger around the edge of her cup till the skin between them stung.

"It was me. I gave him the lift."

The stranger didn't reply. The silence continued.

"If I'd taken him back I'd never have left the place alive."

The boy was under age. She knew what anyone would think, anyone from under a bright Adelaide sky, anyone her mother would have spoken to. But the fear of amputation, bleeding to death in that desert — Her voice had croaked as though it were still afraid. Surely he would agree; surely she couldn't have been expected to go back, even for the hour or two it would have taken.

She looked at the hands encircling her cup. She thought of the cop's hands, his notebook; notebooks and things written forever.

Keough had been there, she remembered. She still owed him five hundred dollars. He could be dead, for all she'd thought of him.

He'd taken her to the opera, given her a painting, made her laugh, treated her like a human being. And she'd abandoned him, too.

She breathed out heavily.

She breathed again, glanced up. The stranger's face an abstract, unreadable, unearthly disc. She wanted to cry out for deliverance from her sins and the punishment they deserved.

"I left him with the cops," she finally mumbled. Her gaze slid back to her hands. "I went to Melbourne. And then I — "

She hadn't done anything. She'd run away and then forgotten.

"Didn't."

The stranger was withdrawing even further. His skin was pale and dry, his long fingers were concerned with the handle of his spoon.

She waved her hands, bewilderment out of Woody Allen to emphasize her harmlessness, her lack of malign intention, the forces of physics and chemistry and geology and history gridded and cross-gridded around both of them like frames, her guiltless inability to have done other than she had.

The stranger positioned his elbows precisely on either side of his cup, steepled his forearms and rubbed his palms over his knuckles. One hand rubbed the other gently.

She was afraid of gentle, devastating treatment.

He put his arms back on the table, hands by his cup.

"You left him with the cops. His parents came. He ran. Ripped his shirt open and left it hanging in his father's hands, to hear him tell it. Then he hid down by the river and that's where I found him." He smiled. "Asleep."

"Moses in the bulrushes." And now to get his attention, forgiveness, she was a Lanie Kazan action figure, biggest torso on the little screen, goodheartednessincarnate.Shedespisedherselfand her self's cravenness; she wanted to withdraw, run again, become distantinvisibleguiltlessinnocent.

"He was scratched and bruised and nearly as cold as death. He was terrified of being sent back. He had to have a place somewhere, clothes, food, a bed."

Her face blushed, ashamed of her.

" 'You're a bleedin' queer, then. Fuck off, you bleedin' ponce.' " The stranger's mouth was cut in rock. "He wasn't pleased when I invited him home. But he didn't want to stay and get mugged or be found by the police." He looked across the table. His gaze lacked the intensity of accusation.

"So I got him back to the flat."

She remembered the hot, black glare that would have been violence if the boy had been taller and stronger.

What could you do with violence but hit back? Why would anyone take it home?

" 'What're you doin' this for? I'm not your fancy-boy.' He'd say things like that every time I turned around. When I made up a bed for him in the living-room, when I cooked, when I got him so much as a singlet or a pair of underpants." There was a quick shifting of light in his eyes and he sat, still, his hands open and his fingers spread, presenting his solid, imaginary world.

" 'Be-cause, Ste-phen.' " The stranger suddenly grinned. "I used to wag my finger at him from across the room. Lord, how he hated that. " 'Because you need it, you little starving goose. Because when I needed help my father wasn't there. Because you're a poor little turd and I'm not, any more. Because I can get you in at the Channel.' He'd scowl and fold his arms and lean back against the wall.

"All through those months he'd stand or pace or hover close to the walls. I was never sure whether he was afraid I'd attack him or whether he was trying to make me throw him out." He shrugged, a small movement. "Half the time I was astounded when I got home and found him still there. I'd given him money. He could've gone into the city any time, gone altogether. Left me nothing."

An echo of desolation in his voice and eyes, and her mother had said something like that once, the same thing, the same way, *what could have happened?* —

"Whenever we watched live local telly I'd talk to him about the lighting and the make-up and how it was all done. He was fascinated. Eventually there was an opening for a cameraman's assistant. Of course he floored 'em at the interview."

The stranger half-smiled.

"I was the cameraman. When he turned out to be as good in front of the camera as he was behind it I made him apply for NIDA." He spread his hands. "Now he's half as famous as God and Russell Crowe and owns a block of flats in Potts Point. His family came and collected him when NIDA accepted him and they all went off to live happily ever after. Well, his father didn't. He had a younger brother, though, cheerful tot. Stephen's set him up in business, bought him a half interest in a pub. When he finished NIDA he asked me to be his manager and agent. He was so good he was offered a lead part in a film in Greece in '82. He was all set to go but asked for a smaller part. Felt he wasn't ready for a lead — and he thought the smaller part was more interesting. On balance I think it was a wise decision."

"But that's it. That's the story."

And so he'd looked at her, dry-skinned and tired, an ordinary man asking her to believe in goodness and poetic justice, and her own contribution to them.

She'd had no idea what to say. She had said yes, and thanks, when he offered her a glossy from his briefcase; she'd tried to rise as he grappled with his coat; she would have offered help or a handshake but her feet were still caught in the base of her chair. And then the stranger was simply gone, papers, briefcase, scarf, coat, still slowly-dripping umbrella. The air and light congealed, felt as late as the dead of night, and she still hadn't replied. She sat in the neon ghost-light listening to the silence of her astonishment, staring at her arms and hands as though she couldn't feel them, staring at the table as though a different heaven and earth could somehow have risen from its surface. The colour and flash of Stephen's life had washed into her own. She'd misunderstood her history and herself.

When she finally stood she put the photo under her coat to keep it from the rain.

(iv)

She unlocked the car, stepped in awkwardly under the steering-wheel. The photo would be bent, she knew, but she could deal with that later; better that than handling it with wet fingers, wiping it across wet lapels to extract it, ruining the matte. She dried her hands on napkins from the glove-box, opened her coat, covered her hands with more napkins and stood the photo against the back of the passenger-seat. When she saw it standing securely on its own she started the engine, turned the lights on, flicked the wipers, pressed the button. A spurt of detergent fell up and onto the glass.

She'd helped Stephen run away.

He'd broken the law.

She'd helped him break the law.

Because of that he'd — got good work, prospered.

Become an artist and prospered. Become someone like Lou Reed, say, who inhabited black T-shirts like the kingdom of heaven, as though he were the kingdom of heaven, dark and magic in his own skin.

In the photo Stephen's glare had become a silky smoulder. He was still a reasonably young man.

To have achieved that so young, settled his family, provided for them, established them out of himself, his own substance and gift —

Another trail of detergent. The windscreen was a smear of thin milk.

The wipers thudded and squeaked.

All her life she'd been a keeper of laws.

If she'd ever breathed freely hillsides would have collided in light the colour of sandpaper. The light would have shattered on open gullies, the basalt rock would have roared and bitten back —

The Adelaide Hills in summer. The landscape of *A Break Away*.

She was the country she'd left. She was the world she'd never inhabited; a shimmer, a heat, a burning.

She'd never turned and become the force she should have been, fire stepping down a dry-grass hill, a sound transforming the air.

The wipers were scraping. She turned them off and tried to slide the gear-stick into reverse.

She'd never walked away.

When she worked at the library she'd read a story about a town that ran on pain and suffering. A child was locked and tortured in a dark room; the rest of the town was light and beautiful, the rest of the citizens happy, loving, long-lived, productive. The child's suffering was the price of their wellbeing.

Most of the citizens were uneasy about the child. The true and only moral heroes couldn't bear the suffering, walked away from the town, found a new place, founded a new order.

She'd never walked away and founded a different kind of city.

But there was nowhere to walk to, her mind

wailed.

She let the clutch out, pushed it back in, found reverse, hauled on the steering-wheel. The gear crunched, held. She backed out, straightened, signalled, looked, drove off.

She'd hated that story.

Salvation was good land somewhere else, open land, land ready and congenial for settlement. What an American notion. Go West Young Man.

It would *take* an American to believe there was good land somewhere else, she muttered, as she'd muttered before when she'd thought about it. Rich, rolling, empty land, open; open to, eye, hand, axe, plough.

She'd wanted to shrug and leave it at that, but that thought had only struck her years afterwards. It hadn't bleached her old, immediate, self-convicting guilt. She'd ended up wanting to flee from her spongy organs and the blood standing upright in the vessels around them because the only decent thing to do was found a different, purer city, and she hadn't and couldn't; had not the slightest desire to found or administer.

The Third World burned or blew away. The First World ran on Third World labour. First

World wages fell until people could only afford what Third World labour produced. Everybody's pension was invested in the companies that built and ran Third World plants and marketed Third World products. Her retirement fund was invested with everyone else's, untouchable, undirectable, beyond her control.

It was still raining: hard, sharp sounds; small, smattery vision. She turned the wipers back on.

And so she was implicated. All the work she did and any work she could do welded her more and more solidly into the chain of exploitation, made her slavery enforce all other enslavement.

The story had won awards.

She jerked the wheel, turned. The night was at the car windows, thick and wet and unbreathable.

She pulled up, watched the traffic lights. "So where *do* you fucking go?" she yelled quietly at the night's glass face. Where could anyone have gone back when the story was written, she continued silently, where could anyone go now?

How had the woman who'd written the story escaped the economy? Was she dead?

The night went on, a tunnel.

The car dipped and bumped between the gutter and her driveway. She coasted along the concrete and braked softly in front of the garage. She breathed out. She was between. She was between home and work, between driving home and being home. These minutes were unscheduled, she could take her time. She could sit and let her mind go blank and watch the rain falling through the glow from the security-lights. Each drop was white, separate, heavy; each drop sounded like softly growing rust. She watched the windscreen, tiny starburst skeletons of ice, tiny skeletons melting. More fell and gathered on the resting wipers.

She glanced at the passenger seat and decided she'd have to leave Stephen's photo where it was.

That Stephen's life and hers had intersected again.

That was a mystery she wanted to take inside, look at, consume herself with, but now she had to leave it out of reach and face the elements of oncoming winter: the steadily solidifying walls of rain, the darkness; the fatigue like a chainmail weight.

She sighed, knowing she sounded like her father. That itself was worth a sigh, she thought, and sighed again, got out of the car, opened the house-door, disarmed the alarm, checked the room. Her old leaf/hand photo prints were still safe on the walls, Tom's prints were still safe on the landing, the cat and the minimal furniture were still safe and here, in front of her.

She still had her hands. She was still a photographer.

She drew the breath she hadn't been aware of holding and smiled at the cat on the couch, the smile almost nothing more than a change in the tension around her eyes; she stepped quickly to the bathroom, struggled out of her coat and put it on its hanger on the ridge behind the shower-head.

The subliminal reflection as she turned past the mirror seemed quite substantial. But she didn't turn back to look. Her mind couldn't recognize death. Her mind couldn't be trusted.

She retraced her steps, stopped to speak softly and smooth and tickle the deep, soft fur at the base of Orphan's ears. The ears flicked; without opening her eyes Orphan stretched a paw and settled deeper into the hollow in the cushion.

She'd never been herself.

She stooped and scooped the mail from the floor under the slot. She put most of it on the low coffee table, opened the padded manila packet she recognized by the stamps and labels. One by one, *F-Stop*, *FreezeFrame*, *Double Take* and *Pulse!* had returned her grainy action-shots of the grandchildren of grunge; tonight *Graphis* had sent them back. She was too tired and preoccupied to feel the usual hot, electric jolt; some other self was weary with failure and grim with disbelief, preparing for argument and asperity. *Rypdal had recommended, had said he would* — And now this: take your Box Brownie and shove it, on stiff, textured, bluecast paper that would display a watermark if she cared to hold it to the light and be impressed; take heed, take note, learn the lesson, and, finally, for their sake if not for hers, stop inflicting her incompetence on the editors of the pillars of culture.

She put the letter on the coffee table, imagined folding it back into its envelope. Someone, anyone, folding it back into its envelope.

She'd felt old when she'd thought of the shoot, a small essay on new, fringe-grunge groups. She'd felt old again later, even in the darkness of the club, even fading into the shadows. She forgot her specially-dyed hair and defended R.E.M. while some drunk middle-schooler with a two-hundred buck geometric accused them of selling out and asked her how fucking old she like her muzak... But none of that had mattered as she shot children to be wept for, luminous white on blackblack, faces boomeranging back into the here and now from a future already dead.

You don't matter if you're not rich, and if you're rich nothing matters at all.

Graphis didn't want them/it/that/her.

Either, apparently.

She peered into the rest of the package. The slides were all there. She stood with them in her hands.

Perhaps Rypdal's rec had annoyed them. Perhaps he hadn't phoned/faxed/emailed after all. Perhaps he was flavourofthemonthnomore this month. His images didn't seem to be circulating as much as they had; offhand she couldn't say how long it was since she'd seen more than one of his cross her desk.

She put the slides and wrappings down, folded the letter. What Editor Wants had been a mystery for twenty years. As she bent to put the envelope down Orphan rubbed against her hand and wrist. She smiled again at the cat, a universe of chance and contingency, the violet blue of her eyes made of atoms created in a star, the star God knew what now, black hole or white dwarf or something beyond the dreams of Hubble. But the cat here, purring, violet-eyed, sweetness and affection and regard.

"The Presidents of the United States sing about you on the radio," she said as she tickled Orphan's neck. "Yes they do. All the Adamses, Tuesday and Wednesday, and all the Roosevelts, too.

"So come on, then." She smiled while she watched the cat focus and make the slight jump to the carpet. "Let's see which Frenzy Stew'n'Chew you should have this evening." She'd checked on the magnesium and salt content of everything in the catfood section. Her cat was old. She was revolted at spending as much on her cat as some people had to spend on themselves. But the cat still had to eat, and the idea of getting poor old Orphan something called Frenzy had simply made her laugh out loud for a second one night, despite her tiredness and the grimy, tumorous Safeway neon.

She and Orphan both had dinner, and when her own snoring woke her she gently moved Orphan off her lap, turned CNN off, checked the locks, climbed upstairs, filed the slides the *Graphis* slushpile pimple had sent back, and went to bed.

Sometime in the night she heard the sound of ferociously heavy rain. She turned over and dreamed. The Space Needle raved and waved its arms. She grunted or moaned or objected and turned over again. A black and white young man who was her father looked across at her and smiled. He always smiled at women, children, battlers. She knew he didn't know who she was. Then his half-tone lawn rose and flew into a nearby darkness.

A weighted movement changed the balance of the mattress. She turned to squint and blink at the clock, found Orphan's shape blocking her view. Orphan always came upstairs in the small hours, trod slowly and heavily on the quilt and settled as a small round warmth.

Sometimes in her half-sleep she felt as though the night were a small personal cave nursing two dim red seeds of life, or was a pair of dark arms curved over them, bearing them along in safety.

But morning's eyes were fragile as opal under water.

Morning always wanted breakfast; breakfast had to be paid for.

"Oh, well," she said, while she smoothed Orphan's warm ears with her fingers and palms. The hair in Orphan's ears was white, as though they alone had been caught in a frost. She'd stared at them stupidly the first time she'd noticed, wondered how the locks had failed and winter had got in.

She sighed, struggled and sat upright, stood and put her heavy dressing gown on, turned and smiled. "Come on, Frailty, Thy Name Is Age, race you downstairs." She watched Orphan slowly walk her front paws down the side of the mattress and take the smallest possible step through the air to the floor. They went down together, slowly, her own feet, at least, still arched and stiff from sleep.

She slammed the door and remembered Stephen's photo.

It was too late, she couldn't go back and get an envelope; she was always breathless, always pinched for time in the mornings. She turned, walked to the car.

Seattle sprawled; it was L.A. without the palm-trees. She could look at the sky on the way to work, she thought, calm down, set her soul to float in the expanse of it —

Because the sky was uncanny.

Somewhere above the cloud-layer there was a distorted orange sun; the air was suddenly red and brown and bronze. The cars on the onramps climbed at gigantic angles, their headlights like magnesium flares — the morning was an ominous Russian icon, a succession of souls hurtling to an electric grey apocalypse in an electric, buzzed-out heaven. The blood in her heart and arms and fingertips wanted to shout: she could have been back in the skies of Friday afternoons when she was twelve and throbbing with hope and joy and the idea of growing into a future larger than the past.

She'd never been.

She glanced at the smouldering gaze of Stephen Black on the front seat beside her, kept wishing she'd remembered to bring an envelope. She didn't want to leave the photo on the seat again, didn't want to drag it naked into work. She'd get an envelope later. Lunchtime. It'd be raining again. The sky was already beginning to darken.

She glanced at the side-mirror, flicked her light, changed lanes.

At this time of year in Sydney the sun poured down like honey.

She glanced at the rearview mirror again. Oh, the sun poured down in northern Canada, unbelievable images of the Rockies, conical mountain peaks dripping light like amber or butterscotch or burnt umber. Here the sunlight might be neither butter nor orange nor honey nor any other branch of ochre. Here sunlight could be rain and the rain came down like galvo.

Her exit sign was a small dark area in the air ahead. She glanced at the mirror again, signalled, and smiled slightly again because the air still faintly tingled (*the sky* is *freedom*, *man*, memory or fiction or some drugwise kid from Woodstock), but now her small tingling of strength came from knowing it was Friday, and from the time she had been seven Friday had meant she was travelling the green and slender land that bordered Saturday. That Saturdays were grim and full of housework never quite changed the bubbling upswell of Friday. Friday the Beatific bade farewell to the monstrosities of the week; Friday the Serene proved that evolution was true, that life is stubborn and full of hope, and hope will prevail over anything if it isn't just too clagged out.

The heavens still buzzed, faintly.

She took the offramp.

A Production and Planning meeting was scheduled for half the morning. The rest of the day would seem quite truncated. Hardly worth bothering with, the sky snake-slither-whispered to her. Leave the filing, go shopping, call your brother at the cheap rates —

Her brother had been fairly reasonable on the phone, winding up their father's estate.

She pulled up, put the handbrake on, turned the headlights and heater and engine off.

She could restart the car now, her blood said, pull out of the lot, go home, call him.

She walked into the building.

Tension; weariness. Two rising flights of stairs in front of her, behind the ground floor stairway the vast dark cavern of Billing and Shipping. She sometimes wondered if it was the cave in her dream.

At the top of the first flight, the first floor: wall of sound, post-it notes like a storm of yellow dandruff; somewhere in the middle the receptionist and a headset, twelve phonelines in and rolling over to the account-execs one after the other, the account-execs bawling because the voicemail was fucked again; the receptionist's assistant, there was one this week, chasing the senior exec while he headed off to the second floor to the researchers and the light-tables *ten calls a dozen fifteen calls from Chiat-Weiden-Publicis this morning, they need sexy legs+lips+hair yesterday, an hour ago, all our jobs're on the line now right now, right fucking now* — but Bruendorf the Senior Account Executive was well and truly ascended and out of mere assistant-range and the assistant was turning back, barrelling into her en passant and flinging herself, tattoos, hair, lipstick, choker, into the receptionist's booth.

She took a breath, lowered her head, hunched her shoulders, clomped upward, turned right at the landing, opened, stepped through, and closed the door on the chaos. She stood in the lunchroom. To compress, decompress, and compress again while a yellow desert of wariness formed and dissolved across her collarbones and ribs, and her shoulders resettled defensively. Torn and curling safety posters, yesterday's *PostIntelligence*, *Wall Street Journal*, *Washington Post* and *New York Times*, next month's *Graphis* and an attendant host of also glossy but nonetheless lesser monstrances of the Image Bidness, yesterday's microwaved spaghetti and salmon reincarnated as today's permanent resident odour, every day's old, chipped, stained laminex —

She'd never been —

She didn't want to go to the meeting.

Even the air rushing down through the passages of her nose knew there was no earthly way in this building, with this routine, this mode of being, this gravity-warp and black hole of a current procedure, to redeem the time already wasted. Of course, in that event, her nose snorted, pushing the same air back, the only thing to do was waste even more.

P&P meetings had become nightmares of blame.

She took another deep breath, hung her coat on the coat-rack, put her lunch in the fridge and stepped out, back into the big room, shout and clutter, circus of researchers at the light-tables and files, Bruendorf with his most recent crisis *State Capitols! White House! Blah-blah! No-o-www!* and Dirk, she could tell by the timbre, dispassionately, *They only do half a mill a year, fuck 'em*, followed inevitably by Bruendorf's rising scream and Julian, she could tell by the change in timbre, loud, sardonic, *Real agencies* celebrate *new accounts*. Jodi, in charge of the table, looking pained, Jodi trying to look as though she hadn't heard and finally, she, herself, M. Miller, at her own desk, chair, headphones.

Dirk and Julian, leatherboys all, had made her a Matador sampler. (For your Patti Smith sneer, dear, Julian had said. While she closed her eyes and outlasted the Adelaidean shame of being seen as someone who sneered.) She still had her Portland library of Machaut, Glass, Reich, Palestrina and Beethoven, Bach and Bowie and Stones and Nine Inch Nails; she could tune in the alt-rock station, crank the volume and raise a wall of Villonified lyrics and guitar-god dissonance between herself and the wailing and gnashing of teeth. And so, quietly, sip at sweetness, survive.

Yes. She could do that for another day, survive.

She waved sketchily to the researchers, put her bag under her desk. There was only an hour till the meeting, not enough time to set up at the data entry terminal.

The figures were ready, the folder in her drawer.

She drew the trays of new and returning slides towards her, took out her jeweller's loupe, put her headphones on.

She took one last glance at the window, felt a chill crawl along her arms. The world was already an opaque grey falling of water.

(v)

She was a permanent, resident, alien.

The thought came to her every time she approached the door of Conference Room A. It was in the approach to the room, knowing what was to come; it was in the room itself, the windowless walls, the airlessness; it was in the continued, unchanged existence of the room every time she walked out of it, knowing it would remain unchanged despite the fact that everyone found it utterly inadequate — too small to walk around in, too heavily furnished to stand upright in, too intimate to do anything in but sit, gaze, and then drop the gaze it would be belligerent to maintain, and so be induced to surrender, one by one, reason, variance, colour, passion, richness, personality, life. The room was conceptually descended from the oubliette or the Old Melbourne Gaol, she'd said to Julian once when they were laughing momentarily about something else; in modern Australia it would have contravened health regulations. She'd never left it without feeling that even her teeth were scared.

"Argentina was a labyrinth of rooms like this," Julian had said, black angry eyes glaring back. "This is how it would begin." She'd looked back, unmoved. She'd told herself he was being a drama queen, as always, or joking, as he often was. She hadn't understood or believed him. She'd been afraid to, she realized, because this morning her mind had taken one look at the room and seen, chilled and plainly, that it was the room in the story; all it lacked was a visibly incarcerated child.

But even while she was astonished at her sudden clarity she realized her body was now bathed in a fine, hot, sweat; she nearly swayed with dizziness as she half-stood to move her chair sideways and make more space, looked down and took slow, invisible breaths.

Last week's red squiggles still zagged across the whiteboard behind the researchers who had filtered in and were wrestling the chairs so they could sit. She wondered whose psychic blood it had been.

She glanced at the doorway and Kringler wasn't there. Rypdal was. *Rypdal* was waiting for the last arrivals. Though she was suddenly chilled to the bone, so chilled the air was drawing in, was the colour of gunmetal around her eyes, she was pleased. Rypdal, who'd hired her, whose grin was benevolent lightning.

(vi)

The researchers were all assembled, aliens, dual citizens, or the children thereof. Nowhere is anywhere, she thought; *here* is contingent, a fleeting alliance. The shuffling of chairs had left her opposite Anh, long black hair, long black fringe, half a dozen silver rings on any three fingers, on her neck a Cleopatran asp of a choker. A young image-maker to watch, according to the *SeaTac Weekly*. She wondered how the rings fared in the developing-trays. Oh, stop it, she said to herself. Send your grunge-pics to the *Tacky*. Make a whole twenty-five bucks.

Rypdal closed the door and stepped to the head of the table. She hadn't really realized he was back in town; he looked tired, as though he'd got in last night or this morning.

Kringler wasn't late. Kringler wouldn't be here at all.

She could have whooped and hollered like a

cigar-chewing conventioneer. Kringler was down in L.A., arranging another infusion of cash into the business. Kringler was gone, halleluiah, was fourteen hundred myalls from his home. Family connections, the researchers said; Hollywood money, according to the account-execs; his gunrunning cousins, according to Shipping. She'd cackled at the savage extravagance of the tales and then felt mildly incredulous and ill at the thought of more Kringlers, Kringlers-to-the-rescue, Kringlers-in-waiting, family photo-albums of ever-more Kringlers, somewhere.

Else.

Ha! There wouldn't be any actual berating and humiliating at the meeting this week! She turned her gaze to the front of the room and tried to look sombre, clear-sighted, preoccupied with the heavy matters that had brought them together.

Rypdal seemed to pause to read the air's intestines, then pushed a stack of printouts down the table, each page face down, pencilled name on the blank side. She guided hers to her and let it lie beneath her folder. She'd found over the last few weeks that the worst thing she could do was look at her stats; she'd learnt to file without reading. Bend with the wind, she told herself, go with the flow, become tears in rain: your stats will never be good again, not till the Viking Portable Stock Agency's no longer on your list of duties.

She'd been stuck with creating the catalogue on CD-ROM, the StokView Image Bank cross-referenced and cross-indexed to a fare-thee-well: each subject-list led to another; every slide was to be indexed by subject(s), photographer, date or approximate date and place of original exposure, photo type and concept(s). Every slide had to be pulled physically from its sleeve and have this information verified and hand-entered into the new database. By her, in between filing all new slides from the photographers they represented and re-filing the normal daily returns which fell onto her desk like endless snow.

Business was booming. The database was permanently due yesterday.

The Problem was Kringler.

Kringler, the permanently on-site partner, The Human Pyramid, The Kraken Wakes. Kringler wouldn't OK a single temp, let alone the raft of temps the Portable Viking required. Kringler's contribution was to lumber through the building unpredictably, threaten to crack the light-tables he leant on, or the faces/bones/frontal lobes/skin-blood-nerves of whoever he was screaming at:

"If you're working less than 60 hours a week you're a parasite! If you aren't coming in Saturday and Sunday the door's over there. Right fucking there! You can leave now! Right fucking now! There's the fucking door, get your ass out, I'll cut your fucking check right motherfucking here!"

The saving grace was that Kringler didn't do payroll.

Whether she was astounded or alarmed was a matter of whether she heard his latest claims (Kringler was teaching them photography, giving them thousands of hours of valuable training) or saw his latest foam-flecked fit (these sparrow-boned interns, that month's receptionist).

The Leathers simply laughed. They were the First Responders; they were afraid Kringler'd have a seizure and they'd have to give him CPR, save his life. She laughed with them, debated how long they should wait, what degree of brain damage they should passively inflict.

"Put him in a wheelchair. He can drool on himself."

"Stephen Hawking's in a wheelchair."

"He's a high-end crip."

"That's a high-end chair."

"Regular chair."

"No voicebox."

"No Depends. No colo-bag."

"Just jello in shit."

She marvelled at their certainty, the way they could draw thick black lines between what they would support and what they wouldn't. She boggled at the brio of Julian's diamante crotch-buckles, the whole swift flash and dazzle of the Leathers' combined psychic armour. She was always uneasy about what might happen and what she might be forced to hear, what she might suddenly look up and find herself seeing.

Which didn't help with The Viking Portable Stock Agency. Kringler wouldn't OK any help. The slave already on the payroll was supposed to magick the data out of thin air, do everything and the impossible on top of that, then assume the position. Figuratively speaking. Some nights she drove home all but murderous with rage.

She suddenly wondered what arrangement of mirrors it would take for Kringler to see his penis.

Rypdal caught her eye. His face was lined and bleak. She looked down, wrapped her feet around the chair legs and covered her cheeks and mouth with her hand. Conference Room A was no place for smirking.

But today Kringler was gone, couldn't possibly burst through the door and her joy at his absence could have fuelled another apocalypse.

She took a breath and made her eyes serious again. Rypdal was waiting, as she knew he would. The man and the photographer proceeded the same way, waited for the subject to step forward into its own time and dimension, for the layered gleam on the golden Buddha's toe to build itself up shadowline by shadowline, the trees to impose themselves mass by mass on the mist. Now he was waiting for the silence in the room to coalesce, present itself as a table. On which he would then lay the stats, images out, used, billed, notable contracts upcoming, and then, finally, The Problem.

The Problem was not Kringler, Id Monster to the Industry. The Problem was The Viking Portable

Stock Agency's lack of significant progress. The Problem was M. Miller, Spastic Librarian.

She was bathed in sweat again, a small, hot fear. She liked Rypdal. She admired his photos. She wanted his respect for what she did.

She wanted at least one temp to do the actual data entry. Then she could check the info on the slide and the state of the celluloid before giving it to the temp to be entered into the database and fine-sorted so she herself could re-file it with the filing at large, and so integrate the construction of the database into the regular traffic. Images were consistently misfiled. Images misfiled were images that couldn't be found. Images that couldn't be found were images that couldn't earn revenue, she said. One point five million slides should be able to keep them all in tea and bikkies, she'd said and said and said.

The faces along the table were masks. She was still sweating. This would be the sixth or seventh iteration of the situation. It was obvious nobody wanted to hear her say it all again. She didn't want to look incompetent; she didn't want to be incompetent — And she'd brought the latest figures so she could say it all again, and saying it all again would convict her of incompetence in all the young, pitiless eyes, in the sorrowful maternal eyes, in Rypdal's glittering-laser eyes. She'd stopped going to lunch; she worked an extra hour or more every night. For the last month she'd been working three hours a day on weekends. She was still as far behind as she had been all along; Kringler still screamed and spat; the situation continued. Uselessly, needlessly, changelessly, dangerously.

Once again she looked towards the head of the table.

She was a permanent, resident, alien.

(vii)

She finished by saying that if the CD-ROM were to make any money they'd have to sink money into it first.

"There's nothing in the budget for more staff." Rypdal, grim.

Budget meetings were above her level, of course. Above Rypdal's too, for all she knew, for all that

Rypdal was a partner. He was always in Bangkok or the Ginza or Tierra del Fuego.

Rypdal looked around generally, then at her. "So what's the problem? Re-filing images returned by customers or entering image-info into the database?"

She spread her hands.

"Both. Because I have to do both and so I can't do either adequately."

"Don't the researchers re-file?" He looked at Jodi.

She knew what Jodi's reaction would be. Jodi's mind had the precision of a civil engineer's but her driving passion was motherhood: Jodi the Head Researcher was not going to see her brood's pull-&-bill stats suffer. The researchers would therefore not re-file, not if Jodi had anything to do with it, and certainly not for the sake of a silent, unattached, middle-aged woman who was neither a mother herself nor Jodi's surrogate child.

Not. Ever.

She often wondered what StokView would have been like to work at if Jodi's kids had avoided early sex and court-ordered child support and gone to college. The researchers had done exactly that, been obedient and ambitious and justified their mothers. For that they had Jodi's undying nurture and influence and support. Some days Jodi's bland imperturbability in the face of the growing tangle and strangle in the cabinets, at the very root of their ability to deliver the goods, make money and so stay employed, damn near drove her to gibbering.

There was nothing to be done. Sometimes she went outside and stomped around the block on her morning break, raved where no one could hear; if she stayed in the building she gritted her teeth and turned up the volume on her headphones. Who could forbid affinity, or alter the demarcations of departments?

She put her elbows back on the table, her hands back over her mouth, shifted infinitesimally. She wanted to watch Jodi answer this question.

Jodi looked concerned, frowned, sounded hesitant.

"The researchers only really have time to re-file what they decide not to send out. With all the new orders they don't really have time for anything else."

Rypdal's eyes laser points, his lips thin. The problem could have been a badly-registered 4-colour separation of the room. "How many images are we talking about?"

She unlimbered her own lips and tongue and teeth. "Five to ten percent of what I find is badly out of place."

Jodi ran P&P meetings when neither Kringler nor Rypdal were there. She waited.

Jodi fixed her with a soft, steady gaze, a soft voice, a complete performance of sympathetic listening.

"That's not too bad. There's always going to be something misfiled."

She marvelled at the steely separation of expression and agenda Jodi managed to achieve, wished she had the gift, the genes. All she had was a barely contained asperity.

"Firstly, they're the categories in highest demand. Secondly, the longer we misfile the harder it'll be to find a greater and greater proportion of images."

"I agree with you. We need more researchers. If we had more researchers then each one would have more time to re-file."

"It isn't a matter of a small, permanent five percent. This is a *cumulative* problem. We could easily get to where twenty percent of our images are virtually lost. And can't earn. We'd be sending out constantly degrading sets of choices. The customers are going to notice. We aren't the only shop, even in Seattle. FedEx goes everywhere."

"But all the other agencies will be in the same position." Regan at work, being Jodi's toady.

"Only if all the other agencies are run by the same howling fuckwits."

The scream would have lifted her out of her chair but she managed, managed, managed to sweat and hold her tongue, let the berserker rage flash through her arteries and leak away.

Jodi, Head Researcher, was in the throes of the last great hormonal flare before the guttering of early old age. Regan had avoided unprotected sex and gone to college. Regan, star trainee, was Jodi's surrogate child and mid-life love. Regan's mother had spent twenty-five years telling Regan she was the least of daughters; Jodi told Regan she was the most amazing of researchers. Jodi was Regan's surrogate mother and mentor and adolescent crush. The thing was *folie à deux* and one of the most tedious relationships she'd ever had to overhear, but it was also a nexus impossible to break through, or past.

"We'll end up losing customers." Her mouth moved again. God, to be anywhere but here, saying this. Her eyes took in the extent of the blankness on the faces, Anh, Regan, even Julian, Dave, Dirk, Zara.

OK. I give up, she thought. Never again. I will shut up and stop filing and just enter data till my fingers are stubs and my lips have knitted together and trapped my tongue behind them.

Rypdal held up his hand.

She glanced momentarily at the tabletop — flat, stiffbrown, grained, she was the table, was laid out on the table — This was it. She took a breath. This moment was the reason she hated any meeting, all meetings. This was the moment when the whole costume and pretence of participation was stripped away and it was clear the gathering was there to be told what to do, to go away and do it and find the door, right fucking there, if they failed.

She was sweating. I'm running like a tap, she thought, I feel sick.

"Has any of this tested out?" Rypdal's nose and stubble and jaw square as a doorframe. Rypdal's eyes holding all the sudden swivelled gazes. Rypdal and the meeting weren't finished.

No one said anything.

"The researchers will spend an extra half-hour a day re-filing. We'll try it for 5 days. We'll have another meeting this time next week, see if that's helped any."

She sighed to herself, stretched her legs minimally, tried to ease her aching knees. The blow had been delivered one moment later than usual. That was all.

Rypdal looked down the table at her. She knew he was going to want all her figures to date as well as the ones from the coming week. Quick and thorough, two more of Rypdal's virtues. Sudden death if you didn't perform. The third.

He hadn't rec'd her slides. She knew it, looking at him, could tell by an absence of vibe.

Mad. Misconceived. Pretentious. Amateur.

Contemptible.

She held her breath to kill her pain and fear.

Regan didn't look happy, mouth a pursed pout. Well might the little slug, she thought; Regan was the one who'd taken the *Grands Tetons* label at face value and filled the Montana sleeves with nude Thai mud-wrestling. Not that Regan had ever apologized or anything. Regan didn't speak to people who couldn't advance her career.

"So if that's all?" Rypdal looking down the two lines of faces.

"Next Friday's the day after Thanksgiving." Dirk.

"The following Monday, then. Anything else?"

No one seemed inclined.

"OK."

They all got up awkwardly, the chair-legs tipping and catching and refusing to move as they always did. She took the opportunity to avoid whatever looks the researchers might be giving her.

She knew they'd screw the filing up royally. Prevention and revenge.

The CD-ROM meant the customers would do their own research, order by email and specify images by barcode. The only jobs left would be filing, pull and return. The researchers would be kept on, some of them, as clerks. At fifty cents to two dollars an hour less. Like herself.

Anything the researchers could do to white-ant that little scheme would certainly be done. She wondered if Rypdal had figured that out.

And then she wondered why Rypdal had backed her up at all. It was the last thing she'd expected.

She stepped into the big room and the two newest account-execs were at the slide-files *Publicis want innercityscapes+urbancanyons+homeboyhabitat right fucking now* and Jodi had sent Julian to head them off and Bruendorf's pounding was coming up the stairs and the phones had rolled over to Jodi's extension and her own desk was an optical vomit of overflowing trays and the rain was still at the windows and nothing was visible beyond it but the brick wall of the next building.

After the meeting she'd normally scan slides for re-filing. It was something she could do while she recovered.

She was unsettled because the meeting hadn't been as traumatic as usual. But this kind of rain meant she couldn't leave the building even though she didn't want to sit. Was she so used to bloodletting on Friday mornings she was lost without it? Life as wartime, the meeting the terror that punctuated the boredom? Was that it?

She still felt vaguely queasy.

She sighed and scooped and stacked the accumulated slides, sat, put on her headphones, refastened her loupe, began to scan celluloid. With the headphones on and the volume loud enough life could be normal again — account-execs could criss-cross the floor, shouting, splattering cappuccino on the grimy sky-grey shag, she could be subliminally annoyed by the stains and the inadequate cleaning, Julian or Dirk could grin and bellow "Scratch!" as he passed, point to the location of some minute fissure in the emulsion of the image in her hand and imply, at the top of his lungs, that he could see from fifteen feet away what she had not yet seen close up.

Well, Julian could see; Dirk only pretended to see... What?

That she was feeble and incompetent, fit only to file and not research?

She closed her eyes, breathed. The queasiness ebbed.

No, she decided. She was being paranoid.

Julian really was extraordinary and Dirk wanted to be like him. Dirk was a kid; it was a game to him. They both grabbed the slides they liked, took them away to look at and debate and marvel and argue over; they put them back in her tray later, or filed them. She'd asked them not to, she had to keep track of the numbers, and of the slides themselves, if it came to that; or at least let her know if they were taking stuff. They forgot, of course, or shone her on.

They'd never yet found a piece of damage she would've missed. Competence wasn't the subtext there.

The girls never said anything about what she actually did. She assumed she was a future they didn't want to think about.

She finished checking the slide in her hand, put it down, took off her headphone and loupe, rolled her neck and shoulders. If Jodi's table was doing four hours' worth of filing today, she could scan these and then put them into the database.

She nudged the empty trays for incomings to the far right side of her desk, replaced her loupe and headphones, and adjusted the volume.

The slides were done. One of Rypdal's had come in; she wondered sourly what use the world of advertising had found for it this time.

She stood, stripped off the loupe and phones. Her back and shoulders and neck were aching.

Anh and Regan were at the cabinets and light-tables, preciosity and pout and territoriality of elbows, Simmel the Too Cool in Lou Reed Exec Lookalike, and some child she hadn't seen before, looked about fourteen — had they hired another account-exec since ten o'clock? Simmel and the child were moving from Jodi's table to the cabinets, so no, they weren't staying, Simmel was smiling and asking them something and Regan was smiling, of course, and no, no one introduces the Slide Librarian, her chief weapon is surprise, surprise and fear; but at least Bruendorf was now off this floor, if not back in his hole.

Her upper arms ached. Her skin was itchy; she felt an almost alien presence under it, slabbed, inchoate, murmurous, suppressed.

She clamped her jaw, closed her eyes, and waited. A frightening sea of pinpoint faces, voiceless forces of fury and loathing winked out at her and then returned to the dark.

She opened her eyes and stood, angered by contact with anger, shaken, frightened. She breathed again, made herself impassive.

At the end of all that, she was still standing at her desk. Between her desk and the windows the air was the same as before, the colour of rain.

If there had been some way, some method or moment of letting peace and calm emerge luminously from the heart of silence here, she could have gone on indefinitely trying to pull a function out of this knot of furnishings and fiefdoms and cross-purposes; she could have gone on trying to introduce a deep silk calm into the slamdunk grabbing of images, gone on trying to give value for money, give sense and value to their own activity. She could have survived on the unintended airiness of the unconverted area of the warehouse, Cake and Cobain and Fun Lovin' Criminals, the occasional blinding summer glimpse of the curves and bluffs and varying blues of Elliott Bay as they appeared through the summer air, and her own ribcage lying along the windlanes with them, companion to that other large creature, the coast —

She could have gone on.

Despite the child locked in the other room?

Her desktop visible between alphabetized trays; dark grey, gouged, scratched, brittle rubber.

How she would have loved to kill the story and the memory of the story, the smug, insistent voice she took for the voice of the woman who'd written it.

Despite the Indonesian girl, the one in this re-filing tray, Rypdal's third most famous slide: a young girl in Indonesia whose hair was capped in a red and white bandanna, who used to live in the rainforest but now lived in a compound of old Nissan huts at night and in a prefab factory by day, whose fingers barely cleared the electric-fast needle of the old industrial sweatshop machine she sat at while a dark river of denim flowed from the needle and thread, out and across the oceans and roads and paddocks, to the discount warehouses she, herself, bought from.

She had looked at the girl's eyes. The girl had looked into hers. She had been chilled and ashamed and alarmed, because she knew that if there had been enough peace and quiet light at

StokView she wouldn't have cared. She could have kept on quite happily even despite the slavery that dressed her in the denim overshirt she was wearing right now; that would go on dressing her because she couldn't afford anything else.

So. Yes, then, she said to the woman's voice. Even despite the girl in Rypdal's slide, even despite the child in the story.

She worked at StokView. She had to earn a living; there were fewer and fewer places to do it.

Where did the starving masses of her needs think they could all survive? In the job-market for the female over-50s?

The surface of her skin suddenly radiated heat. Dave and Zara were at the cabinets, at the tables, at the beginning of the alphabet.

She hefted the alphabetically-last slide-tray. Her skin intimated sweat. She carried the tray to the cabinets.

The rain was another language, pittering at the window.

(viii)

She.

Didn't.

Want.

To.

Scurry. Any more. Through the endless closed loop of the world where all rooms were the same room, all jobs were the same job, all slavery enforced and guaranteed all other slavery.

She had to be somewhere else, look at something else. At the escape of Stephen Black — almost into the kind of film she'd almost seen being made on Barry Keough's island — and then to Sydney Harbour.

She was starving for something else, to wear a black t-shirt, to be in the Kingdom of Heaven, to be herself, tobegone —

She set the slide-tray on top of the first cabinet, opened the fifth at SY, found SYDNEY, dropped the sleeves onto the lightbox.

Depths and shadings of blue in the windows of the towers in the sky, angled visions of other windows, another sea —

The jumpjerk shock; fear, chill, resettling.

Into the room she was in, in the head and body she was in, after the shock of seeing the pictures she'd taken when Tom had been alive.

The slides were still full of a vivid golden light, a moving serpent. There were other pictures, the shadows in the room where they stayed, the spinnaker of blue-white illumination from a northern window.

She scanned the labels in the sleeve again, set the sleeve aside and face down, and scanned the next.

Early mornings, late afternoons.

She finally began filing from the tray she'd brought, occasionally transposing images, sometimes re-filing entire runs until she reached the end of the Ts. If she got a clear go at it, she thought, came in early, left late, maybe just devoted lunchtimes to it, she could finish clear through MC by the end of next week, and then when she was finished the drawers would glide like silk on their runners and close with a whispering kiss, and she could turn to her desk across the room and be unfearful for the time it took to get there, the memory of that silky glide the only reachable equivalent of the Sydney she'd been in and the home she'd had with Tom for a moment, that standing, air-filled realm of light, that mediaeval heaven interwoven with earthly air.

No.

She couldn't.

She wasn't fixing the alphabet this week, she was applying barcodes to plastic strips and doing data entry, CD-ROMing as hard as possible. A flash of panic: she still had half a tray of slides to file.

Escape was a myth. Escape through the mind was a myth. The idea of an equivalent of escape kept her imprisoned, teased her along in the room that was irreparably connected to the room in the story, the room that kept this room built and inhabited.

She climbed upright, balanced, percussively assisted the bottom drawer to closure, turned and glared at the clock. Five minutes and she'd go to lunch whether the slides were done or not, and bugger all of corporate America if they thought they'd see her back here in an hour. Or even in an hour and a half.

She grabbed S-R of what was left — SALEM,

OR, SALEM, MA, SALAMIS, SACRAMENTO, SABLE, RYUKU, RWANDA —

She frowned. There were no empty horizontal rows, suggesting that other images were with a client. There was nothing. She flipped through the entire drawer. Perhaps someone had given Rypdal his own hangers, made it easy to pull his stuff since it was in and out so much, not the kind of thing a researcher would normally bother to do, but maybe someone had, Jodi, the Leathers —

Nothing.

She got a few new hangers from the supply-cupboard, dropped the Rypdal into a slot, dropped the other new hangers in, finished the rest of S and R. She looked through the drawers above and below RW-. Nothing. She scanned HIMALAYA by photographer, ditto CAMBODIA. She found a total of two images, both out of order. Apart from that a massive absence.

She went back to her desk in a daze, tidied, got her bag.

"Going to lunch."

She caught Jodi's eye and nodded and gestured to let her know that anything from Shipping was just to go into her trays.

She couldn't stay in the building; she had to get out even if the bloody air had turned to bloody water.

The slides were her responsibility. Rypdal's had disappeared. All but three of them.

Were simply not there.

She went into the lunchroom, put her coat on, was almost overcome with heat, shivered.

She didn't know where to start.

She couldn't look at a million labels, she didn't have time —

Shipping! She could check the records. The invoices were itemized. She could tell Carla she was looking for something a customer said had never been sent. She took her coat off again.

She spent an hour. Apart from the three slides she had gathered herself, nothing of Rypdal's had gone out in the last six weeks.

"Chris?"

She stood at his office door, trying not to look as catastrophe-ridden as she felt. Rypdal looked up from his laptop, recognized her, didn't smile.

"Er, can I ask you something?"

She stepped through the door, closed it.

Still no PC, she thought. The posters on his wall were old. *Photonica*, stunning, but old.

Rypdal was a focused suspension of hollow-sea eyes, prickling stubble, hair.

She folded her arms, dug her fingers into the flesh over the elbows; she half-registered the grain in the veneer on his desk, her skin and stomach repelled by the unchanging ugliness.

"I don't know what's happened. I don't even know how to say this."

Her responsibility.

"I can't find your slides. In the collection. Only three. And nothing of yours has been invoiced for six weeks. I checked Shipping."

She looked up. She was ready to offer him her resignation. Lost slides — She was costing the man his livelihood. Christ only knew how much she'd cost the company.

Rypdal was absolutely still. His eyes flicked to the door and back. Not one other muscle moved.

"I don't know how it happened. I don't even know how I didn't pick it up earlier, that none of your material was coming back in."

Rypdal closed the laptop, unplugged it, coiled the cord around the adaptor, put the whole assemblage into its carry-case. He stood, slid around the end of the desk, opened the door with one hand, awkwardly gestured at her with the other while the carry-case still swung from it. She scuttled out. He primed the lock, pulled the door until it secured.

"We're going to lunch."

She ran, got her coat. Rypdal gestured to indicate the pair of them to the storm of noise, post-its, turmoil, receptionist; he struggled into his coat and hurried her down the stairs, leant against the front door, opened it with his weight, let her get through and out into the hard pewter lances of the rain, nodded her past the cold, dripping statue of Chief Seattle, bronze turned grey in the dank, dark-washed, brushed-steel light.

The local cafe was long and dim, divided into two rooms. No one could see in from the street, no one could see from the door to their table. A Sinatra song on the CD jukebox, in her ears, around her, a smooth warm coat of a voice from a world no one could live in any more.

Lunch was over. Rypdal ordered beer and a communal plate of fries because fries were still available; she ordered tea. Rypdal appeared to have a tab, she thought, and lowered her rainhood, set her coat to drape on her shoulders. Her hands were icy.

Rypdal looked around. "This is the only dive around here not owned by someone from Microsoft." He looked back at her. "So it's only the last six weeks that nothing of mine has shipped?"

"Seems to be."

"Did you check Kringler's?"

She twisted her lips and shook her head. "Only skimmed the invoices looking for your code. Didn't actually focus on anything else."

"But you're sure nothing of mine went out."

"Pretty sure."

She should have taken longer, she thought, but she'd been gone that hour and now this time as well.

She'd never catch up. Finding stray slides in the cabinets would be a huge job, and even now the trays on her desk would be spilling with more.

The fries arrived, huge segments of potato, skin still rough and dark on the outer curve.

"And all my images are gone." Rypdal hadn't touched the fries or his beer; he kept his left hand on the wetwet waterproof laptop case. An old guy from the bar, cardigan, slippers, walking-stick, went to the jukebox.

"They're not where they should be, or anywhere close. Not by name, not by subject. Both sets seem to be gone, name and subject. I don't know that they're not somewhere. I didn't check every drawer.

"Couldn't. Not in that amount of time. I can't now, not in the kind of time I've got today. Unless I came in over the weekend? I could do that."

"No."

"I don't know how it happened. I can pay for new dupes. I don't think I can repay your lost — "

"Oh." His hand brushed the air, dispersed the suggestion. "No. Check the files for Kringler's images. Let me know what you find."

Rypdal stood and strode towards the door. She left her tea, grabbed her bag, pulled up her rainhood and followed, stepping through the beginning of a Billie Holiday song.

(ix)

Her desktop was a mass of little dark squares in little white frames.

She stood, put one tray on her chair, cleared a space in the other, rough-sorted until she had more space, pulled the Ks, fine-sorted them. In the drawers there were plenty of slides under Kringler, plenty of empty slots. His stuff was clearly both in stock and in circulation. She jotted down a quick count of the numbers. The back of her neck prickled. She didn't think it would be a good idea to go straight to Rypdal. He was someone she hardly ever saw or dealt with; she'd already been to lunch with him today, publicly, after he'd unexpectedly supported her. She didn't need more atmospheres, suspicions, rumours, ambiguities.

She barcoded and typed solidly until the windows were dark walls of small, sticky rain and she was the only body in the room and her eyes and shoulders were killing her. It wasn't that late, she knew; people tended to try and leave early on

Fridays, actually did if Kringler wasn't around. But even so, Orphan would be starving and she herself hadn't eaten, for all that she'd been to lunch.

She folded the note for Rypdal, tidied her desk, put her raincoat on, went downstairs.

Rypdal's door was open, his light was on. She detoured. He looked up from his laptop.

"Glad I found you. Here." She took the note out of her pocket. "As of this afternoon or right now."

He held his hand out, took the note, read it.

"Thanks."

She waited to be told what she'd found, or what it meant, be sent off with some sort of notion as to the extent of her culpability and the repairs she'd need to make.

She had to make amends.

But the man between the old posters and the dirty beige sheetrock walls was closing his laptop. As she watched, she saw he was also closing down, attention, spirit, force, presence — he was becoming colder, stone-like, was wearing Rypdal's skin and bones and frame and face, but wasn't Rypdal.

"Have you eaten?"

He looked at her as though he had to translate

from a huge remove or a dead language.

"Dinner?"

Skeletal, fossil. She was afraid for him.

"You could have dinner at my place." Gently, softly, making the air around him soft because he was brittle and breakable.

"It'll only be soup and bread and stuff like that."

He nodded. He locked up, she signed out. It was still raining, but the drops were, superheavy, supercooled; over and around and beyond the ominously heavy drops there was a hollow, listening cold.

"It isn't far."

She had a bottle of whisky. She'd bought it her first winter here to make the weather less appalling. It hadn't worked. But, she thought, Rypdal could have some hearty soup and real bread and tea or coffee or a tot of whisky, be sustained, be restored enough to take off safely in his all-terrain assault vehicle. She'd go to bed, Orphan would hold the universe steady with her weight and they could both sleep in the generosity of a cave of healing darkness and be borne forward into a small calm day. She could call Rypdal then if she had to, see if he was all right.

If she had to go in to work afterwards at least it would be quiet and she could concentrate, work in 90-minute cycles, check the files or get immense amounts of bar-coding done and not be totally fried. Go in Sunday, too, if she had to. Though, Lord, she was sick of having to.

"Are you sure?" Even his voice sounded dry, a membrane abandoned by an outgoing tide.

The raindrops had spines now, visible on the windshields of the cars still there.

"We still have to sort out what you want done about your slides."

Her hands were freezing.

"Hm." He paused. "Where do you live?"

"Bit south of Chinatown. Fifteen minutes."

"Gentrification Central."

"Yeah." That had been something else in the Indonesian girl's eyes.

She turned and left Rypdal to walk to his Jeep.

Kept his headlights in her rear-view mirror.

They stopped on the way; she bought groceries and cat-food. She smiled, bleakly, momentarily; Tom had loved that supermarket chain, always marched in, pranced as he shopped, pounced whooping on the deals originally aimed at the unemployed PhDs of SoCal. The shop you loved your only tangible monument, she thought as she ducked back into her car, even in the late, scattered mind of your wife. Lord, she thought, the appropriations of a mercantile culture, as she stopped smiling, slid Stephen's photo one-end other-end into the plastic bags she'd purloined, and buckled up.

Signalled, started to drive.

"Help yourself."

The lounge-room was eerie, the laptop screen an odd, luminous emanation on the coffee table, laptop and Rypdal a small separate duoform creature, a body hunched like a question-mark joined by arms to a private flickering god or demon or oracle, the whole continuum like an ancient sculpture of unknown origin, uncertain ritual significance. She turned away as though it were some kind of subliminal menace.

She'd hung their dripping coats, found him an extension-cord and outlet and given him the whisky bottle and a glass.

"There's ice." She called from the kitchen. Gone to ice-fur and frizzle, she remembered. She crossed her fingers.

"No. Thanks." He'd poured himself an inch of whisky without taking his eyes off the screen.

She clattered with pots, dishes, toaster. She hadn't had visitors since she left the Book Group and declared to Orphan it was quite clear she could neither read nor cook nor have a conversation.

Orphan was hiding.

She took a bowl of food upstairs, called in a whisper at the slightly open closet door and left the bowl by a furry, hollowed-out pile of t-shirts. A small desperate duoform creature, she thought, a body curved as a cuphook joined by arms to the absence of a fur-bearing particle of warmth and sanity and life in itself, the whole image to be called *The Widow Waits*. She snorted. The idea was almost as twee as the Book Group's novels.

She was on the other end of the futon-sofa with a half-inch of whisky in a glass of her own. Rypdal was still communing with his oracle.

"Do you want me to go in tomorrow?"

"No." Rypdal turned from the screen. "You haven't lost the slides. They've been removed."

Rypdal sitting, rigid and unmoving, staring at the screen; sitting, ill-dressed and unmarried as any priest.

The rain at the window behind them, behind the wall behind them.

"StokView originally had three partners. When we bought Jacob Rix's share of the company I raised cash on everything. Sold my house. Sold most of my gear. Jake was old. He'd been good to me. He was a great photographer."

As though the words came from his spine or fingertips, some repository of complex but present-tense functioning. His eyes were as expressionless as his face.

"I've got a museum-piece Technica of his. Apart from that I own an old Leica, two Nikons, and an antique Jeep. I rent a rat-hole. I don't have one red cent of liquidity."

She suddenly wished she were drinking something that didn't waste its time on flavour. Vodka, maybe, something that would go straight to her danger and alarm centres, activate them.

"But what's that got to do with your slides?"

"Jake was old and sick. His images weren't making money. He wanted to retire. I was well-known; the agency has exclusive rights to my stuff. That was keeping us going at the time. Kringler came from *National Geographic.* That's where we met. Good photographer, always on assignment, but not a real high flier. So with Jake sick the logical one to drop a photographic career and run the business was Kringler. He takes good stock. That swimming-pool marble pattern is his, the one that looks like dark green steak."

"Know it. Goes in and out like a fuck in a fit, all twenty-seven copies. So do his clouds. He leans out the window to take those." She'd seen him as she passed. For the first time since leaving school she'd thought about centre of gravity and tipping-points. Tip, tip, tip. Oooh, splatterboss.

She moistened her throat with grog, poured herself some more. Such a substantial taste in the mouth.

"We also get a lot of income from news under license. We sell everything, L.A. riot flames for new gas fireplaces — "

She'd heard, she'd seen, the Leathers had told her. She'd shuddered, horrified, as she'd sat in front of CNN while L.A. went up in flames and National Guard enforced a curfew and the Army ringed the city with regular troops. Tom standing on the sand at Hermosa Beach, talking about the Watts riots, the National Guard, eighteen years old, jittery with adrenaline and fear, prickling with sweat and apprehension and bayonets, marching with their bayonets fixed, skitter-nerves down the streets of South Central and little kids running up to them and the kids' mothers in the doorways crying and crying and calling the little kids back and the kids not seeing any danger at all, just guys who might give them gum.

She'd watched and seen it happening again: another cohort of terrified Guard recruits and the massive snafu of a split command. Christ, the bloodbath it could have been.

The riot flames were still burning. They were just in peoples' eyes.

The fire next time.

A sound of the rain on the window.

"Very weird things end up happening with images." Rypdal coughed, a sharp sound, angular and hoarse as a dog barking.

But the caravan moved on, she thought. None of them would be here if it didn't.

Rypdal's lips were still the same colour as his cheeks; his eyes looked brittle. He scarcely blinked. He moved his gaze from his hands to the screen, the screen to his hands. The screen flickered with changes, convolutions.

The whisky in her glass was the same colour as the wood veneer on the coffee table.

She didn't want to take on Rypdal's mind and burdens. She owed the man her job and occupation, then, still; that was all. She didn't know what that could ultimately entail or be made to entail. But she'd already obviously implicitly offered something; she'd brought him home.

Rypdal was utterly still, staring at the screen. She could imagine him turning to stone.

She didn't know what she had to do.

She turned her glass, now that it was in her hand. She was ambivalent about whisky still, the warm sting that sharpened and shadowed other pain just before dulling the mind and everything else.

Past Rypdal's sitting figure she watched Orphan suddenly catch sight of him, crouch, lengthen herself, flatten her ears and tail, turn and run back upstairs. She smiled slightly. There oughtta be postcards, she thought. *Wish I were there.*

Rypdal's silence also lengthened.

"The point." She was tired. Her body was beginning to feel like wet cement.

He turned the bleached, fixed lenses of his eyes to her, gestured at the bottle.

"Sure."

He replaced the cap, turned. "If one of us fails to bring in more than twenty percent of the gross income in any given quarter, and the imbalance continues the following quarter, he forfeits his share.

"If I don't bring in more than twenty percent of the income over two consecutive quarters, Kringler gets the company."

"Oh."

He turned the laptop. "Here."

She stood and bent, hands on knees, squinted, saw a pie chart in blue, pink, purple, green, fawn, and variants.

"This is the income-split among the top ten earners."

She straightened and put her glass back on the

table, bent again and blinked and peered, seemed to see less the longer she looked. The angle was wrong, the screen was small.

"And here." He keyed. A bar graph this time, the same hideous colours. "The historical view." He pointed, fingernail against the quilted, nonreflective glass.

"Why was it set up that way?"

"Jacob Rix. We'd been carrying him for about a year. The way it was set up back then, the income was split evenly between us all. We thought that would be pretty much the way it would be generated. After we bought Jacob out we set it up this way. No one would have to carry anyone else. No one would go broke raising buy-out."

She stared at the screen again. Her eyes felt like hot holes. She caught herself wanting to pour another grog and knock it back like cough syrup, force entry into some sort of understanding.

"But your slides —" She could imagine them at the bottom of the cabinets, under the bottom drawer of one of the rows where they'd fallen, got wedged, got chewed up by the metal edges, the poor little celluloid wings. She still couldn't quite see how they'd got there, all the hundreds of them dead in a sort of worldwide collapse of butterflies and lightweight things. Yes, she thought, slides did remind her of wings. They always almost fluttered when they fell.

"Kringler pulled them."

Her mind was a crater. Edges of shock sluggishly rolling down and into her arms.

Jagged splashes of process as she tried to imagine.

Baby imaginary hands mimicking. Slides being removed.

Dulled nausea; fear and outrage slowed by hard liquor.

"But how could he expect no one to know? Someone would know they were missing. They can't just all disappear and nobody know. I found out after six weeks and they'd have to be gone for months. And you'd be checking the figures."

"I'd scheduled two long assignments back to back. Last week I changed plans, flew in early; I'm due out again Tuesday. You're the only one who regularly checks the filing, and you wouldn't figure it out because you're going to be fired for not getting the CD-ROM data done."

The air was a burr, a high-pitched whine, a fever.

No, she was the fever.

"But I keep telling the meeting I can't get it done. I've been telling them for two months."

"There's a notice of verbal warning in your file."

"A *what?*"

Jodi kept those files. What the hell — Of course, she'd put anything into them she was told to. And she wasn't the only one with access. Kringler had access. So did Rypdal. He'd been at them this afternoon himself, obviously. Implied he had.

Jodi at the meeting. Jodi would have run the meeting if Rypdal hadn't been there. Jodi's eyes into hers, concerned. The slow delivery of the message, Jodi trying to warn her?

Stop checking the filing.

Jesus!

"You won't be in the CD-ROM! I'll be barcoding stuff as it comes back. The most-used stuff will go into the database first and we'll play catch-up later."

Rypdal blinked, eyes opaque, a sandy sea.

"No. Whoever replaces you will be told mine will be done separately, later. A new hire wouldn't see any problem with that."

She looked at Rypdal's eyes. Who could she

trust when her mind thought the dead were alive, presented her with them, and not the dead she cared about?

She couldn't think. Her mind was running from side to side in its own picture of her brain, doing all the running her body couldn't.

"Why are you telling me? Why aren't you going straight to Kringler, or your lawyer?"

"Kringler's out of town."

Of course.

"He'd deny it if he were here. Probably say you lost them and fire you for that."

She was all liquid fear. She was caught. She was guilty.

She'd either have to stay and endure it or take a StokView lunch. Go to lunch as usual, never return. Three days later, according to the StokView Death Rites, Bill the Handyman would advance on her stretch of gouged grey rubber desktop and the drawers in rows beneath it, with a gleeful, determined glint in his thin blue eyes and on his thick gold filling; he'd do the same with the fridge in the lunchroom. Bill the Handyman, with the glint in his mouth, would scoop and take whatever photos or drawings or defaced and collaged postcards, action-figures, replicant plastic insects, dinosaurs, angels or tableaux vivants she had mocked or mocked up and hidden away, tokens, totemic fuckyou pieces of resistance, cast them into the non-existence of a black trash bag, then hurl the bag into the company's semi-trailer-sized dumpster. Any lunch-bag or lone food-item marked with her name would go into the small black bag of daily trash.

And no one at StokView would say her name out loud again.

Take a StokView lunch.

She had no idea how people could just walk out like that, just walk away, no medical insurance.

Rypdal didn't seem to think he'd said anything extraordinary. He was adding whisky to his glass, he was putting the glass down; he'd made the screen a vast array of little mustard blobs.

Her skin felt. Weary.

StokView had been relatively small when she'd started there; it had been intent, intense and interesting. Jacob Rix hadn't been gone very long; Rypdal did most of the training. But then Rypdal went back on assignment, the volume of business grew, the number of employees grew, and Kringler's lumbering, panting, ranting, hourly bottom-line requirement grew. Everything grew: Kringler's neuroses grew, the potential for conflict grew. Backgrounds and outcomes entwined, entangled, spat mirrors, duplicates, reverses: Kringler's suicided father doubled with Jodi's suicided mother, the researchers' anorexia played against the programmers' plumpness, the Leathers glowered at the Young Freemasons, film school grads left for gigs at UCLA, account-execs screamed they could sleepwalk through Paris Island. It was appalling. It was fascinating. Without the Leathers it would have eaten her alive.

Everything shrinks but the boss's demands and the cost of living, she muttered to herself, said out loud to the Leathers who were often standing and smoking on the shipping-dock when she returned from her round-the-block slogs and venting rants. Arbeit Macht Frei but Freitag never comes.

It certainly hadn't come lately.

She'd never walked away.

Shit, she thought. She'd walked away three bloody times, to L.A., Portland, Seattle. Even to Athens, if it came to that. Four. Melbourne. Five.

Business was war and employees were the

enemy.

She was afraid to walk away again.

She couldn't walk away again.

She was being fired. There was nowhere to go and she couldn't stay.

She was exhausted. She just wanted to desist, go upstairs and pull the night around her like an old soft dark denim shirt, have the darkness soak up and soothe away the burning of her skin and the sweat it was exuding like a different kind of tear.

She let her head rest on the back of the futon.

She'd dozed. It couldn't've been for more than a moment. But she woke slowly, felt as though her body were still in some layer of the earth, some kind of vastness buried under geological ages.

Rypdal was keying; the graphic she'd seen earlier had gone.

She leant forward, trying to wring some movement out of her earthbound, rockbound self. The screen displayed a table of figures. Rypdal began jotting in a notebook.

"Chris."

He turned. His face looked smaller, as though he had begun to think of himself as an object, something that no longer had a home, couldn't blend or blur into places, spaces.

She touched him on the forearm. "I'm sorry, I'm absolutely exhausted."

He glanced down at her hand, watched while she withdrew it.

He hadn't heard the words, she told herself; only misinterpreted the touch.

"I didn't know if you wanted to drive or stay here. I've got spare blankets —"

He suddenly turned, bent, closed the laptop, packed it away as though he'd been admonished. The back of his neck was red.

Of course he could drive home, she realized. He wasn't a child or stupid aging clerk who had to go to bed early to be able to go to school the next day. He had a jeep, the jeep probably had studded tyres, he'd probably had the tyres fitted the first legal day; he'd been up and down the Andes and Himalayas.

Rypdal was looping the cord. He'd already separated the extension and looped that.

"No, I understand." His voice sounded as though

he'd stopped using it years before. The shadow at his throat looked like a wound.

"You can stay, leave as early as you like. Or we can go out for breakfast, figure out what to do." They'd have go out, there was almost nothing in the cupboards.

His face was bloodless, his eyes thin as glass.

"I think it would be a good idea. You look tired." She made no movement.

Rypdal nodded and put the laptop down. "You could be right." He glanced at the arched opening to the kitchen. "Uh, which way — "

She gestured and then walked ahead of him, turned the bathroom light on and left him to the prospect of white paint and porcelain.

"See you in the morning. Sorry. Goodnight." There was soap. There were towels in the obvious cupboard. She went upstairs, got the second set of sheets, took the second pillow and the top two blankets off the bed, went downstairs, spread the sheets on the futon and left the blankets folded. She hoped he wouldn't stumble into the television or the coffee table as he turned the light out, but she was too tired to hold the thought clearly, or to care.

She saw her father again. The grey grass was a shallow cube. The man and toddler were flat. She waved to her father from her own coloured world but he couldn't see her. Then the two grey figures were in a snowglobe and flew into a suddenly high and spangly dark.

She woke, remembered the globe, drowsed again, turned over, slept and saw a warm, banded and golden sky glowing over a cup of sea and land. She and the spheriscape were one whole, egg and shell, until she half-woke again, growing chill, and felt exiled from home and sea.

She was sad, alarmed, unsettled. She knew she wasn't fully awake; she knew that waking up wouldn't end the anxious aftermath of the dream.

She was wrapped in sweat. She wanted a shower, she wanted to get the sheets into the washing machine. She wanted to go on napping.

But, she supposed, she had to continue the narrative of her life, pick up the thread, find out where she was, what she had to do next, remember what happened yesterday.

She opened her eyes. The room was a cube of snowlight.

Orphan wasn't on the bed. She stretched a bit, breathed out, thought well, she'd get up, find Orphan, feed her. She yawned and lay still, still unmoving. Yesterday was the day beginning with the copper-bronze-grey sky —

Rypdal! Rypdal's slides were missing and Rypdal himself was here, downstairs, sans food or anything.

She grabbed her dressing gown and fled. For a moment she still wondered at the loss and grief her arms had felt as she thought of the sea and the sky and herself, and vaguely, at the back of her mind, wondered at the joy she'd felt before she'd woken and then been cold and afraid.

(x)

Rypdal was in the kitchen, showered, shaved, scrubbed. The whisky bottle was in a corner on the counter, nearly empty, but the glasses were washed and inverted on a paper towel; his bed-clothes were folded and stacked at one end of the futon; his laptop was on the floor next to it.

There was a cell-phone on the stack of bedclothes. Bright and chipper, she thought, calling bright and early — She was glad he was still there, hadn't gone storming off at her rudeness, glad that he'd been busy and not finding her humble abode a waste of time. She was slightly awed at how much he seemed to have recovered, his sheer energy. Imagine getting up every day to do something you wanted to do, she thought; imagine not being under siege. She almost wondered what he'd been saying on the phone, then cringed at the idea of how long he must have been up, waiting for her to appear and be hostly.

She put the kettle on, went voyaging through the

cupboards. She found the week's last two breakfast bars and gave them to him; she wanted to hustle him out to a coffee-shop before he could register her other lacks. She was almost amused at her cage of attitudes — she didn't know the man but she still didn't want him to see she hadn't dusted the tv or the coffeetable since the fourth of July, hadn't cleaned the windows —

"I was looking at your photos earlier."

It was just as well her head was deep among the pasta jars and teabags; her face could set like concrete and not be seen. She didn't want to talk about photos, have to withstand a newscast of judgements. That was another reason she didn't have visitors.

But of course there was no escaping.

"Which ones?" She had the stories ready, the short versions, the fuckoffoutofmylife versions.

"The Sheldrakes."

The back of her head hit the cupboard-frame. When she could breathe the ache and throb into submission she turned and stood.

The kettle was nearly boiling. Rypdal stretched along the shelves that held the inverted coffee-mugs, took one.

"How do you know? How do you know who

took them?"

"I remember the anti-busing shots. I'd seen some of the others back when they were published. He went to high school with my oldest brother."

"Oh."

So as a boy this quasi-stranger might have come to know Tom. Might have come to know her, then, did know her now, didn't really know her at all.

Gordian nots.

Her head was sore. Her mind was an unlit wooden interior. The kettle was coming to the boil.

"So how come you've got Sheldrake prints? How did you find this stuff? He was killed pretty young."

Last night's bread was all gone. The butter in the fridge would be cold and hard as winter.

Bloody life was too bloody hard.

Rypdal turned the screaming kettle off.

"He was my husband."

The silence went on screaming. Stopped.

"You can't have been married long."

"No."

She opened the fridge door, got the milk. The butter was cold and hard. She left it where it was, dropped the bread into the Tiditrash, put milk, sugar, spoons and a selection of tea bags on the counter.

"Help yourself. I'll have a shower and be ready in a few. Sorry. If you want to eat we'll have to go out."

"Hey, no problem." His hands, raised.

She imagined the gesture was an apology for his reflexive, devouring curiosity, for the unmannerly, utterly American interrogation of his host and employee, for his trespass into her provenance. She wondered why he wasn't offering to leave. He could just call to let her know what to do about his slides.

They settled at a table by a window. She watched him continually because, she realized, she relied on her sense of barriers and did not ultimately, necessarily, want them either raised further or breached.

Rypdal seemed cheerful, as though he had a purpose held in temporary suspension, as though an internal clock had begun a several-hour countdown towards the moment when his smile and pleasantries would become the hard, narrow pinpoints in his eyes on workdays.

But for the moment he was simulating humanity

and ordering low-cholesterol eggs.

She waited till the ordering was done.

"So what about all of us? What about the StokView people? The employees? The redefined down to crap povertyjobs? Because that's what the CD-ROM will do to us."

Rypdal's eyes widened.

"Yes," he said. "It will."

"Then what about us?"

He looked at her without changing expression.

"I can't save you from technology. You have no idea what poverty is." He was suddenly vehement.

She thought of his least characteristic shots, crowds in bazaars and favelas, erosion in the land leading up to Nepal. The waitress returned, mug of coffee, cup and saucer, pot of hot water, basket of teabags.

"Poverty spreads. It can spread anywhere, open up anywhere."

"Or we can be made poor."

She dropped an Irish Breakfast bag into the pot.

Why should she let the sensitive soul off? The sensitive soul got to fly around the world photographing poverty. The sensitive soul was a partner, owed loyalty downwards. Rypdal owed them as much as that id-monster Kringler.

He looked directly at her.

"Maybe. But I still can't save you."

She peered into the pot. The teabag had drifted to the surface. She sank it.

"Not from the peaks of the Andes, no. You could try staying here, running the place at a profit. That might keep Kringler out of our personnel jackets, too."

"I'm a photographer, not a businessman."

"Is *that* what you've been telling Kringler all these years? God, you're telling him to screw you."

Where do you get off? she thought. Do you really believe people are allowed to define themselves? Do you really think self-definition can't be self-interest or condescension? She poured a few test-drops, poured again. Choice was a privilege, not a right or an unconscious act; it was privilege as performance.

She sipped. The tea was scalding. Good, she thought from inside the cells of her arms and tongue. Good, the pool of heat said, the cup between her hands, stinging, put down, picked up again.

At one of her temp jobs once, another panicked and sweat-stinking stint in another grey cubicle, they had suffered the visit of a Regional Vice President, power suit, patent leather stilettos, seamed stockings crooked. The Agency formally thanking them.

They all, all the temps, had stood in a semicircle facing makeshift tables. Grotesquely large fake silver trays tilted towards them, full of grotesquely large cookies. The cookies were covered with grotesquely large, dayglo-coloured Smarties.

The Regional Vice President smiled. The temps stood, docile, waiting, staring at the mirrors and beads.

I'd rather keep Manhattan, thanks.

A sphere of radioactive silence centred somewhere between herself and the trays; it ended about two feet past the ring of temps. She'd actually spoken.

She'd seen no reason at all to give the Regional Vice President's local lickspittles an easy time while they told her she'd never temp in this town again, and fired her. She dyed her hair, lied about her age and immediately hired on at Horror Works Agency #2. And then StokView's ad had winked at her from the *PostIntelligence* like The City On The Hill, like Freedom Through Permanence.

Her mouth was burning. She wasn't minding.

Rypdal's eggs arrived. Her pancakes arrived. She attacked them.

But now she was finished at StokView and so she was supposed to scuttle off and start begging for some sort of job again: show up on time, notwearingjeans and notchewinggum, have a positive attitude, include all relevant experience, paid or unpaid, demonstrate eagerness and suitability for whatever the hell it was they paid ten bucks an hour for in Seattle these days, simulate the hermit and the hermit crab in some secondhand cubicle, tape Dilbert cartoons to the pencil-tray inside the drawer inside the desk inside the cage that was tied to all the other cages, call her growing moroseness rebellion, do her best to disguise it because she wouldn't survive her supervisor if she were obvious and wouldn't survive her own despair if she were honest —

The tea was burning.

She didn't care. She took another scalding sip.

She was finished at StokView. Without thinking about it, without wanting to be. She was going to be thrust out, ejected, spat forth.

Once again her life had become a chasm of illusion and waste.

Her old boss the High School Librarian had written to her once and told her what happened to the library after he'd retired. She hadn't known whether to commit murder or mayhem, she'd been so furious at the ruination, the willful destruction of a working organism. Ignorant, unsupervised, slackarsed clerks and ignorant, slackarsed, corrupt administrators. The procedure manuals had been thrown out. The Librarian's procedures were gone, all the appendices she'd added to the manuals herself were gone. The order and balance of the shelves, the meticulously updated and cross-referenced records, the well-watered plants, the opened windows, the dusted books, the known and cared for and mended and groomed breath and circulation of the body of knowledge she and the librarian had laboured to maintain, were gone.

She didn't even want to think about the Film Library. Between the advent of video, funding cuts, privatisation and the psychoses she'd witnessed it might be a blessing if the thing had fallen down some day-of-judgement rabbit-hole. Nothing she'd done would have survived longer than a long weekend; nothing she would have been allowed to do could have de-marginalized the place.

The only significance of her lifetime of work was that she was still alive, drinking scalding black tea like the saddlers, carpenters, coalminers and farmers of her ancestry, like everyone else in the mute, unknown, buried past.

Rypdal was stirring his coffee. She watched his eyes, his eyelashes.

Her pancakes were finished.

People were nothing, she thought, or they were someone like Rypdal, or they were on another level of economy and being altogether, Lou Reed, Laurie Anderson, Bowie, Stephen Black.

But.

She'd helped Stephen Black hitchhike out of hell.

She had done that.

So. Her life had amounted to a contribution to Stephen Black's life. She had done that, and gazed at the light in whatever room she was working in.

She had not gazed at fire, or breathed its air.

She had created order so order could create a

quiet centre and light could take up residence in a room: the same light that descended on mountains and leaves and on worked metal and stone, made forms known to one another, crop and farmer, predator and prey, that had shone on history and would shine on the future, that recreated itself in darkness and became the sharp, focused black and white, velvet black and creamy white or the thick, palette-knife colours that made all life possible. Created a centre so that light could take up residence, be a filling, compensating, redeeming presence.

The steam from the last of her tea was in her nostrils. She could breathe tongues of fire-vapour now.

Well, then, her nostrils said. Her life had been a well-lit chasm of waste.

Her work had been intangible, been ephemeral by nature, or been thrown away.

She breathed out.

It was not enough for a lifetime.

She breathed again.

She glanced through the window. Snow on the ground. She looked back.

Rypdal's eyes were crazed green glass, polished

green serpentine.

She realized he was afraid.

His assets were at risk, his work was missing, his future income had disappeared with it, his half of the firm was at risk.

The waitress refilled Rypdal's coffee-mug, brought her more hot water.

"So, Chris." His jaw immediately set. She'd seen it in passing, blinked and forgotten but still always known: obsession. Not a word she liked levelling at anyone. But not, ultimately, surprising.

"What do you think should happen? About your slides?"

His eggs were finished. He was adding creamer to coffee as though his eyes were photographing every molecule.

His concentration seemed to blur for a second.

"Right now there's only one thing to do. I have one set I can put in place right away. I'll have the originals re-duped over the next few weeks and charge that to the company." The smile on his lips was the bitterest she'd ever seen. "And see Kringler."

She imagined him in Kringler's doorway, a blade,

a rapier of light.

She could be amused by light because she had caught fire.

"I think, for your pain and suffering, you should renegotiate. A non-exclusive deal."

Rypdal's eyes darker, soapstone.

Cold rising off her skin like heat.

"You can't afford to lose StokView income. But you can't keep looking over your shoulder all the time, either. So tell him your stuff's non-exclusive from here on out, or he gets hauled into court. Now."

"Why does he think I'm going to take him to court?"

A black dot was growing on her tongue, the whole dark underside of the world. Her arms and feet were scorched rocks. Her eyes bit back at the air.

"I'll give a deposition saying he told me to take your slides out of circulation."

Rypdal's eyes opaque in a momentary silence. "I'm setting up a website, licensing images for collage, web design, educational use. Jacob Rix's stuff, old stuff from the public domain. I'm talking to everyone with any kind of work that's not tied up. Eventually we'll all have some sort of supplementary income. Maybe something substantial." He pushed his plate and the whole assemblage aside. "Why don't you come in with us?"

Her eyes watched the waitresses carrying huge trays weighed down with pancakes, eggs, ham, hashbrowns, steak; watched the busboys with round brown pots of coffee that turned grey when anyone added milk.

The men of the families coming through the front door might have been machinists from Boeing. SUVs, but none of the sheen of the middle class.

"Because there's no guarantee I could make a living."

Her mouth finished speaking. She still had too few images to shop, even with the black and whites. Her eyes turned back to Rypdal.

"Don't quit your dayjob," he said. Sarcasm and finality, though his face and voice were like a film of ash, as though they had never had anything to do with speaking.

She hadn't meant. To accuse, blaze, burn, and burn him because he was taunting her, suggesting she was afraid to leave her dayjob and believe she could be secure when she knew she couldn't; because his sarcasm made it clear that having a dayjob meant she wasn't anything she wanted to be, wasn't real, not like Rypdal himself, or Tom, or Stephen Black, and now never could be; because he had told her she was losing the very dayjob that kept her unreal but alive and trying to maintain the last ravelling ends of the illusion that if she desired it strongly enough, got up early enough, stayed up late enough, worked hard enough, made an image fine enough and placed it shrewdly enough, and did all that over and over and over again, she could, one day, win —become one of them, a professional, be accepted and redeemed, be left with more than the light in the sky or the gleam on furniture and an inability to capture it as it trembled and breathed.

And it *was* an illusion; it was propaganda and sop: untouchables kept quiet with unprovable blame for past lives, promises of higher reincarnation dependent on their behaviour in this. Or promises of reward for hard work.

She was never going to become one of them. She not only didn't have the time or the energy to produce much, she didn't see the right way. She didn't see the right things.

She watched the skin-textured ash of his face.

She hadn't really meant to burn.

And she didn't quite know how to apologize when he might well not have intended —

She looked down.

Bugger it, said her blackened mouth. Don't apologize. Let him twist. Let the earth and the sky between you go on burning.

So she let her gaze creep out through the window, rise, expand. More SUVs and passenger vans pulling into the lot; the snow being driven on, thinned, made feeble edges of ice, reduced to slush and filth, the people wearing puffy nylon jackets, looking like hot-air balloons. None of the kids were skinny.

When she was a kid on the beach at Glenelg she could count the ribs on most of the other kids. Vegemite, the beforeschool, afterschool diet then. Tom had said there ought to be a Vegemite Cookbook: recommended uses: jungle camouflage, industrial solvent. No one could eat Vegemite, he'd said, let alone get fat on it, it was un-food. The starvation probably stayed for life, he opined as he looked slantwise, heavenwards.

She watched the snow, thought of Glenelg and the small sea-edges smiling on the flat of the sand, the long quiet hiss and ripple of waves on water. Adults got padding and pillows for their birthdays, Tom said. She almost smiled. He'd been such a fool.

There was one kid she'd seen once. She'd always remembered him, no reason at all except that he was a skinny boy running along a beach, knobby knees, ribs, all speed, energy, bone, was a skinny body learning to be hard, designed to inflict and withstand pain, not be penetrable. The Kouros of Apollo at the Getty Museum, skin of stone – Kouros of Aries, that boy had been. Was that when their eyes smashed, she wondered, when Australian skin became stone, just at the edge of puberty? So many Australian men with smashed and broken eyes. One of the occasional frighteningly brilliant people at uni had mentioned it once. She'd noticed it afterwards and then, coming here, she'd forgotten.

Tom himself had been all bone, except that he was warm. His eyes had never been smashed. Until he had been, utterly.

"OK, *don't* quit your day-job."

She jumped, turned, returned. Rypdal's voice still as ashen as his face, his eyes pinpoints.

The Look was back: the only two things in existence: Rypdal and the image he could draw out of mist or chaos.

The waitresses were criss-crossing the room, taking new orders, used plates.

"If you're interested, there's another way of doing it."

His voice a shade more definite. She thought of a single ear of seeded grass on a blackened hillside afterwards, ashless, but still black.

Within her skull she commanded her eyes to arrange some sort of stare.

"Oh? What's that?"

"Replace my slides, say nothing to Kringler, finish the website, leave StokView when we're ready."

The laserpoints of his eyes mapping her skin, reactions. Her eyes refreshed themselves.

We.

She could stay at StokView, leave at her own behest, not be fired, failed, made officially waste. Keep her dayjob's illusions, if she wanted to.

"I'll authorize temps to do the data entry. You can supervise. Having the slides back in circulation will keep the partnership going. My work will automatically be on the CD. Kringler and I renegotiate. Non-exclusive from this point on."

We.

She could be kept on, valued. The cold was overlying a joyful, expanding hope, a hopeful, embarrassed joy. Years of work, she thought, and her latest slides. He wanted them, the slides she had at home, the slides she could produce; he hadn't seen them but if she'd taken them then they were OK, would be OK; she was goodenoughafterall, she was a photographer not an upstart clerk, she was truly the vast other being that had ignored the table and observed the Puget Sound, roots and fingertips, claws and scales-teeth-eyes glittering. She had been all along.

Could be herself, her photos, her own country. Rypdal was saying so.

She could be herself, fire; Rypdal was saying so. Now, after a lifetime of insult.

Her eyes were a black centre of burning. She was inside a globe of fire, circled by fire. The fire turned its attention to the air and spoke.

"What have I got that you want?"

"Tom Sheldrake's last images. His name. There's a partnership in the web business, if you want it.

I can't offer you much upfront because I may not have much. I borrowed against my half of StokView for the design work and licensing."

Aeons of falling.

The depths of her chill, skin to bone.

(xi)

She walked out behind him, barely aware of the slush.

She was nothing to him, not even a clerk. He'd walk right through her to get to Tom's work, walk through the living and draft the dead to raise money for Jacob Rix.

Rypdal turned. "I called Sygma this morning. Their files show nothing from Tom Sheldrake for two months before his death. All the other rights have reverted. The entire catalogue is ripe for marketing."

Yes, she knew. Tom had been getting around to it. They'd both been busy, in the subtropical sunsets, the mornings and afternoons, the too-few nights.

(xii)

They'd come back to her condo so Rypdal could get his gear, his neat little laptop, his neat little fold-up phone, his honest professional's neat little old and battered jeep.

So he could look at the negs.

She'd stopped and shopped because she needed to be able to set one foot in front of the other without Rypdal's presence, pressure, interference.

So that she could flex her wings, fold her wings, settle, be nobody, somebody, nobody – So she could feel like herself, be whatever she was, not be a description. Not be Rypdal's description.

So. They were back. Rypdal had one of the beers she'd picked up to deflect his attention. He was standing against the counter next to the sink, drinking from the bottle; she was on her knees, stacking food into cupboards and the fridge, building a structure that wouldn't collapse the minute she closed the door. She was doing small things because she couldn't imagine or manage large ones.

She blinked and focused again. She didn't know how to end the day or the situation or the conversation or the silence.

"How many Sheldrakes do you have?"

She turned. "About eighty rolls. Like that. Developed but never printed."

Rypdal had massaged the celluloid out of its black canister, was still holding it up to the light, tilting it to illuminate the silver. She'd almost expected to see him fish a loupe out of his pocket and comment on micro-tears. He hadn't said anything.

She finished with the cupboards. She stood, rolled her neck and shoulders, sighed and opened the freezer. She still didn't know what to say to him. She squinted at the ice-cube trays, washed and wiped them, poured bottled water into the small cubic hollows. She stacked the trays, closed the door to the freezing compartment, caught sight of the strip of sky above the cafe curtains as she turned to face the room —

The sky was the same colour as the overlapping shadows at the side of the stove; she was standing in zones of colour, layers of sediment, sky to floor. Renoir had been right, she thought. In a hierarchy horizontality was all; class was the great reality.

Silence.

She moved to the counter by the sink, started folding the grocery bags.

"A career in themselves, depending on the images."

Rypdal, neg in one hand, beer in the other, film canister on the breakfast bar beside him. Rypdal accusing her, implying she'd refused to promote Tom's images, kept him from his rightful place, buried him a second time. When she'd clutched them, kept them to her, kept them safe —

When she was letting him look at them so he could market them!

She looked at him, eyes, face, eyes; felt her eyes and the sky darken.

"I couldn't cut the negs."

Dead cold, her skin almost separate from her, a distinct thing stretching, a lamination of fever and chill. "Apart from anything else, I have a negative genius for sales."

So much heat she ached.

"Wait. We've had this conversation before. About marketing. Was I going to rec some stuff for you? Did I forget to do that?"

"If you have to ask me then you must've." The heat on her skin almost audible. She hadnoenergyforthis.

"I'm sorry. That was not my intention."

Rypdal's renewed attentiontothismatter like a great wave gathered in the upper shadows of the room. Rypdal being told of imperfection, wanting to flood imperfection away.

She leant against the cupboards, let his gaze pass. Her fingernails were claws. She wished they could tear her skin, let her step out of the fire.

She shrugged. "You were gone. But I'm not sure a rec would have made any difference. But thanks." Her smile taking her by surprise.

His lack of response taking her by surprise.

Her skin calming, mute and weightless again, undetectable. Her tongue resting in her mouth.

Rypdal nodded. "You said you had eighty rolls of these?"

"About that."

"All black and white?"

"Some colour. Slides. A few rolls. I'm not even sure what they are."

"OK."

But she could still see the dark wave poised.

She turned her back on it, took the folded bags off the counter, crossed the room, began layering them into the bottom drawer of the cabinet beside the stove.

"So what do you want to do?"

She didn't know.

She'd never known what to *decide*, *declare*, *do*.

And now Rypdal was demanding she demonstrate her skill with the d-words she'd never been able to manage because she'd never imagined she could shape or control the world or her place in it, and that was the kind of control that kind of question assumed. There was only a wave ready to drown her in the leatherbound cave she dreaded and dreamed about.

Compared to a man like him she'd never done anything: looked after her cat and kept her house, flattened brown paper bags and put them in a drawer. She could see her mother's hands now, flattening clean, wrinkled greaseproof paper into the broken basket at the bottom of the cupboard beside the sink; her mother's hands hanging clothes on the line, her own hands offering pegs.

That was what she did. That was the kind of thing she did, meekly turning up to work every day, driving along the same set course, her hands becoming her mother's on the steering-wheel.

But Stephen Black by the side of the road, torn to blurs by the rain.

But her hands in watery solution, cream and black and velvet depths taking shape under them, images emerging to sharpness; sharpness preserved in matte as she turned to peg and hang them —

Turned towards Tom, the sunset behind him, her mouth open, her skin, her body open all at once, speechless at what she could almost touch.

Her hands making a collage: a longhaired, white-haired woman locked in a house of grief and loss, her hands changing and making the image. Herself outside it, unconstrained.

Stephen Black's photo protected in plastic on the counter above her head.

She did do things.

The things she did had consequences.

Tom had danced and capered around her. Tom had wanted her and her killer eye even if it hadn't killed much lately —

She was not quite nothing.

Even in Rypdal's terms.

Even in her mother's terms.

She jiggled the drawer back into place, pulled herself up, stood.

Rypdal closing the canister, putting it on the counter, turning, leaning; Rypdal's arms stiff as wood, extending down to the counter behind him. She thought of crucifixes; she thought of the layers of gold and wear on the Buddha's toe in that incredibly famous photo. Impact was Rypdal's subject, she realized. The other slide that had made his rep: the Dalai Lama by a fax machine, wearing a deep red robe, bending toward whitewhite pages —

She wasn't interested just in impact.

She wanted to be everywhere, like air. Around the image, behind it, off to the side. That was what she wanted to do and be. Be everywhere, blaze.

Collage.

She turned and washed her hands, dried them.

It didn't matter what Rypdal saw when he looked at her house with its minimal furniture and widowhood and cat. She wasn't Rypdal's agenda; he wasn't hers.

She was herself.

She didn't have to acquiesce. She was not nothing.

But Rypdal was also right. She was also Tom's

executor.

She hung the towel, turned.

"The negs OK?"

Rypdal being right was looking at his watch.

A flash of bright red across a dark field. Her nerves liquid, electric, herself furious, fed up.

"Look, Chris. You see Sheldrake prints on my wall while I'm asleep, and before I wake up you're on the horn to Sygma. You offer me some sort of deal and you want it settled in three minutes. Give me some room and some goddam respect!"

Rypdal looking up, body still, compact.

"You can't just take what you want out of my life and then act as though you haven't even got time to speak to me. If it weren't for me you wouldn't know what Kringler's done, let alone that these images exist."

Still silence. His face still grey.

"I'm sorry." His eyes, skin, body, remote, withdrawing. From what? From dominance to parity? She didn't know.

"I guess I tend to push. I find things don't happen if I don't make them happen. We can discuss this later."

A small shrug.

"It's up to you. Nothing can happen until I see how the negs print up."

Taking away her chance to even taste the idea of publishing Tom's work with some sort of gravity and prestige, of being *the one who published his work* — Skin hotcoldhot, fear to illness to airborne fury —

"How they'll print up! That's insulting! They're *Sheldrakes*, you prideful little shit!" But her arms hadn't moved, her lips hadn't opened. Somewhere a crisp of ash hung suspended, hot and dead.

Rypdal looked at his watch again. "It's late. I have a prior."

All pretence to conversation between equals utterly lost.

In the still, furious settling cold she was done with StokView, done with all of them.

Don't let me keep you, she was tempted to say, but the sarcasm would have been lost. Men like Rypdal never saw themselves as being subject to the judgement of clerks.

"I don't want to keep you" – a reptilian tongue, segmented, supple, scaled, lay in her mouth with darkness and stalactite teeth, the sea a memory out past the rocks, pale and notional.

"But these are Sheldrakes. They'll print up. That's not a negotiating point. The negotiation will be about rights and permissions. You can't do a bait and switch. You can't offer and take away. We will negotiate or we won't, but we will not be speaking as though the work itself might be *iffy*."

Metal tongue, parrot tongue, round and segmented, will and wyrm to itself. Withdrew while she waited to be able to coalesce, know who she was now, where she was.

Rypdal blinked.

"You're right. I'm sorry. You're right. I guess I was killing the messenger. Kringler, Pete —" He drew another breath.

"Peter Kringler and I covered El Salvador and the Falklands together. Then we founded the company. During the first Gulf War he asked me to take one of his cameras. Jake was sick and Pete had to stay here and take care of the business."

Pallor, brittleness. He was almost loquacious. He was still in shock, she realized.

"I'm sorry. It's fine." She smiled and stepped away from the counter. "We can talk about this some other time." She moved forward and out of the kitchen, wasn't quite showing him out, wasn't quite not – It was like moving parents from the classroom on Parents' Night, her skin whispered.

Rypdal gathering his laptop and cellphone and keys, the keys jingling.

She felt some cold heart in some cold star turn its back.

Then Rypdal was stepping through the front door, taking glasses from his vest pocket, climbing into the jeep, looking back suddenly, eyes ovoid, photogrey —

She waved uncertainly.

He raised his hand briefly. Without thinking she smiled the old smile, as though they were engaged in a collusive magic, potency, charm, luck, assurance; as though the sky were electric, buzzing with joy and hope.

Rypdal started the engine. The sky died back into passivity.

(xiii)

She stepped inside, closed the door.

The room was empty.

She'd been right to be afraid when the Leathers merely laughed.

Cold fear trickled down her scalp.

Rypdal would never forgive her: she had seen what Kringler had done and done to him, seen him in complete shock and at a loss, and at *that* moment she'd demanded parity.

A small weight pulled at her ankle. Orphan was brushing against her. She bent and stroked her and picked her up, tickled the ears of love and fragility and interdependence. She rocked the cat and stared past her to the floor, wondered what she had finally and irascibly done, what softness or camaraderie had just become impossible.

The same camaraderie she'd started out with, she muttered. The myth of it. None.

(xiv)

She drove to work. She drove home.

There was nowhere to walk to, no newer, purer city to find or found. That was the lie the story told. Imprisonment was everywhere. It ran through the world like the colour of blood.

(xv)

Rypdal was gone, back on assignment. If he was around at all he nodded from a distance. They never spoke.

Tom's negatives sat on her breakfast bar.

(xvi)

The ancestor serpent round and golden and flowing along Johnson Street, Kew, opening the sky and the earth beneath the asphalt, all glimmering firelight and waterlight, quicksilver capillaries —

She took a breath.

She didn't have to stay at StokView any more. Nobody cared what she was. She didn't have to, either. She could be a fire-breathing dragon, a dinosaur, a used up widow, a cat-owning mouse, a scorched, post-volcanic hillside, a breath within light, or nothing at all. Nobody cared. It didn't matter.

That was her freedom.

(xvii)

She'd exercise the privilege she had.

Been forced to.

Have.

She'd sell the condo, be and make her own country, the landscape she'd imprinted on, Third or Fourth or Fifth World or whatever it was now, nation, colony, suffering tectonic plate, infestation of humanity, land become quarry, quarry become pit on the wrong side of the postindustrial divide, contaminated pissedin proteinsoup reflection of the qantasleap to post-Millennial, post-material habitats; she'd go home to cathedrals of air, scouring wind, the silence of stilled voices, land become pit, dirt, stones, fragmentation; to nation become states become regions, areas, fields, zones breaking down to stone, earth, loam, leach; to word become hyphen, hyphen crushed to newlynamed entity, splinter, particle; and through it and over it all the serpent shimmering, air in air, choked on words and roads, living and dying in the cities' shattering canyons, cracking asphalt like the tips of soursobs —

(xviii)

She'd buy as little as possible, enslave as few as possible.

She'd take her leaf-prints, and Tom's pictures, and Orphan, and she'd work in the quiet and available light in a room in Glenelg, grains of sand on a polished wood floor, wind straight up off Antarctica; she'd photograph the serpent and work, do what she'd started to do: pull images out of the light and the crumbling city and the earth and the darkness in herself, and build them, put them on the web with Tom's, and let their images stand there together, blazing; love, memory, protest, defiance, desire.

M. F. McAuliffe was born & educated in Adelaide and Melbourne, has an Honours degree in English & graduate work in photography, film, & anthropology. In 2002 she co-founded the multi-lingual, award-winning, Portland-based magazine, *Gobshite Quarterly* with RV Branham, & continues there as contributing editor.

She made her US debut in Damon Knight's *Clarion Awards*, & has since co-authored *Fighting Monsters* (with Judith Steele, Melbourne, 1998), the artist's book *Golems Waiting Redux* (with Daniel Duford, Portland, 2011), & supplied the libretto for La Mama Courthouse's production *Orpheus: an Australian Tragedy* (Carlton, 2000); the text of *Crucifix i.*, along with a photograph, appear in the Yoko Ono-curated installation, "Arising", 7 Oct., 2016 through 5 Feb., 2017, at Reykjavik Art Museum. She is currently editing & publishing some titles for Reprobate/GobQ Books.

a **shoegaze** book

we'll meet again...
don't know how, don't know when...

www.ingramcontent.com/pod-product-compliance
Ingram Content Group UK Ltd.
Pitfield, Milton Keynes, MK11 3LW, UK
UKHW041842200726
13854UKWH00005BA/1986
9781944244415